KU-489-983

Brainse Bhaile Thormod   Tel. 6269324
Ballyfermot Library

SPECIAL MESSAGE TO READERS

THE ULVERSCROFT FOUNDATION
(registered UK charity number 264873)

was established in 1972 to provide funds for research, diagnosis and treatment of eye diseases. Examples of major projects funded by the Ulverscroft Foundation are:-

- The Children's Eye Unit at Moorfields Eye Hospital, London
- The Ulverscroft Children's Eye Unit at Great Ormond Street Hospital for Sick Children
- Funding research into eye diseases and treatment at the Department of Ophthalmology, University of Leicester
- The Ulverscroft Vision Research Group, Institute of Child Health
- Twin operating theatres at the Western Ophthalmic Hospital, London
- The Chair of Ophthalmology at the Royal Australian College of Ophthalmologists

You can help further the work of the Foundation by making a donation or leaving a legacy. Every contribution is gratefully received. If you would like to help support the Foundation or require further information, please contact:

THE ULVERSCROFT FOUNDATION
The Green, Bradgate Road, Anstey
Leicester LE7 7FU, England
Tel: (0116) 236 4325
website: www.foundation.ulverscroft.com

A GRAVE AFFAIR

When Edmund Burke, MP meets the woman he loves on a sunny afternoon, he cannot know that it is for the last time, or that a brilliant career is about to collapse in a scandal of murder and blackmail. Edmund, deep in negotiations that promise peace in the Middle East, is a target of nationalist fanatics who will stop at nothing to remove the main obstacle to their success. And he's about to discover where the loyalties of friends and family lie, as the police cast their net ever closer . . .

SHELLEY SMITH

A GRAVE AFFAIR

Complete and Unabridged

LINFORD
Leicester

First published in Great Britain

First Linford Edition
published 2020

Copyright © 1971 by Shelley Smith
All rights reserved

A catalogue record for this book is available
from the British Library.

ISBN 978–1–4448–4405–4

Published by
F. A. Thorpe (Publishing)
Anstey, Leicestershire

Set by Words & Graphics Ltd.
Anstey, Leicestershire
Printed and bound in Great Britain by
T. J. International Ltd., Padstow, Cornwall

This book is printed on acid-free paper

1

Saturday morning, The Fox was pretty crowded. The weather was glorious after yesterday's rain, and half the customers had taken their drinks into the yard and were sitting perched on the walls enjoying the sunshine. It was the sort of day when it was good to be alive — not a day to die.

The Fox lay almost exactly halfway between London and Brighton in the sleepy country town of Horsham. The light in the saloon bar passed dimly through the small paned windows of Georgian glass. To anyone in sunglasses, like the young woman who had just entered, it must have been like stumbling into a cinema. The woman with blue hair sitting in the window wondered how she could see to read the paper she was holding before her face.

The girl and the woman were the only two people on their own. Mrs. Richards

Leabharlanna Poibli Chathair Bhaile Átha Cliath
Dublin City Public Libraries

had been sitting in the window since opening time, watching the cars drive in and quietly downing gin-and-tonics as she waited. She was a woman on the sad side of forty. She had noticed the girl as soon as she came in, not only because she was young and lovely but because Mrs. Richards had a feeling that there was something oddly familiar about her; only, those enormous black glasses of hers masked half her face. Everything about her was simple and very expensive, her only ornament a black silver-decorated cross hanging below her breast from a silver chain; and yet the plain white dress with the black accessories was not quite what one would wear in the country. A film star, Mrs. Richards hazarded, and at once saw the absurdity of that. Who had ever seen a film star without her retinue?

Even the men at the bar had turned to gaze at her with a certain curiosity, a slight stirring of lustful interest; only, it wouldn't have been considered quite the thing to have started chatting her up, for the men leaning against the bar were the serious drinkers, the habitués. The girl had taken her drink to a table by the wall. She folded back her paper.

Mrs. Richards noticed her sitting there with the one drink for a long time. So for all her youth and loveliness, she was waiting for someone too. Mrs. Richards felt a kind of pity for her. *Not one of us is spared*, she thought, setting down her empty glass. She glanced up as a group at a table rose and left. It was gone one, and people were beginning to break it up. She might as well go home too. It was obvious he wasn't coming now. She had known all along he wouldn't, though her heart had refused to acknowledge it. A woman of her age knew when an affair was over. Mrs. Richards stared down into her empty glass, her heart like lead in her breast. Her head jerked instinctively back to the window at the sound of a car racing up the slope into the yard, like one of those wretched animals subjected in the cause of science to continual electric shocks. Mrs. Richards could no more help her response to the stimulus of this particular sound than they could.

But this time, too, it was not the car she was hoping for.

It was a Bentley, and out of it stepped a slight fair-haired man in a check cotton shirt and blue pants. Despite his casual youthful air, Mrs. Richards observed as he entered the saloon that he was older than he appeared at first glance. About her own age, she imagined with a tiny flicker of interest; of hope. But alas, he took no notice of her — or anyone else — but made straight for the bar. A pity, for he had a kind face, a nice face, rather like — oh, she couldn't remember what his post was, but one of the men in the cabinet, except that this chap was smaller and younger.

The solitary young woman had departed. Mrs. Richards saw her stalking delicately across the yard in her stilt-like black sandals to the lime-green Cortina. But once inside the car, she simply continued to sit there, unmoving, as though she could not make up her mind where to go from there. She removed her sunglasses and studied her face in her compact mirror, touching it up, smoothing her hair.

Mrs. Richards, gathering up her shopping basket with the avocado pear, the prawns and fillets of sole which now she would never bother to cook, knew exactly how she felt. Except that Mrs. Richards had nowhere else to go but her lonely flat, and no other prospect ahead of her but the rest of this day and all of Sunday somehow to be got through.

Outside, car doors slammed shut. People called out last-minute hilarities. The serried vehicles edged to and fro, in a sort of motor-quadrille. The green Cortina slid into position with a toot and the Bentley graciously backed away. For a moment, the girl in the Cortina glanced at the man in the Bentley and their eyes met; then the wheel turned in her slim hands and she shot away. The Bentley, on the other hand, continued backing up to the far end, stopping beside the archway which led to the toilets. A large white dog jumped over the seat and scrambled out after his master, waggling his hindquarters and leaping to embrace him with yelps of ecstasy.

'Down, Beau, down! Good dog! Good Bobo!' He took from the back seat the dog's tartan rug and draped it over his arm, locking the car doors before the dog was allowed to drag him away, pulling the man sharply to a halt again each time it paused to sniff earnestly at some interesting brick or tyre or flowerpot or wall and lift its leg as a sort of P.S. to whatever message it found there. In this half-brisk half-desultory manner, they walked towards the Causeway.

A pale lime-green car was parked on the left hand side. Mrs. Richards, crossing the road on her way home, saw the man stop to say something to the driver, and then the door opened and dog and man got in. She caught a glimpse of the girl in the white dress, and recognised with a sense of shock that this was a pick-up, a common pick-up. Mrs. Richards, who would have been just as ready to leap into bed with the gentleman if he had looked her way, was stabbed by a sharp pang compounded of envy and unbearable loneliness. Tears pricked her eyes, dazzling her, as she meandered homewards, unsteadied by gin and self-pity.

She was thinking shamefully, as she put her key in the door, of ringing Larry on some pretext or other for the last time, when out of nowhere she suddenly recollected who the girl was. It was Alys da Sylva.

★ ★ ★

'Are we allowed in? We've brought our rug,' the man said as he stopped beside the Cortina; and the girl, smiling, had answered, 'Of course.'

The rug was thrown onto the back seat and the great dog obediently climbed on to it. 'What a handsome fellow he is,' said the young woman, patting him as he climbed past. 'You never told me you had a dog. What is he?'

'Beau? He's a Pyrenean mountain dog. He belongs to Cynthia, really.'

'Ah!'

'How beautiful you're looking,' the man murmured, gazing at her. 'It's wonderful to see you again. How I've missed you!'

'Then you're not too annoyed with me for ringing?' she said, with a melting sideways glance from her beautiful dark eyes. 'I had the impression that you weren't too pleased to hear me.'

'That's only my telephone voice. Behind my curt manner beats the same mushy old heart you know of old.'

She laughed. 'Darling, it's lovely to see you.' She reached out for his hand and threaded her fingers tightly through his. 'And I take it as a high compliment that you should make the time to see me.'

'It was, I admit, rather difficult.' He turned her hand over and planted a kiss in the palm and then gently returned it to the steering wheel. 'Shall we go?'

'Where to?' she asked, switching on the ignition.

'Anywhere not too far away.' He hesitated to say bluntly that he hadn't much time at his disposal. But she evidently understood.

'You didn't mention you had a new car,' he remarked as she drove. 'For a moment, I thought you hadn't turned up when I didn't see the old Vitesse outside.'

'Would you have been very angry?'

'I'd have killed you!'

'What I like about you, Edmund, is your courtly old-world chivalry,' she laughed. 'How's Cynthia?'

'Very well, thank you,' he said quickly. He never liked her to talk about Cynthia. Alys was well aware of this taboo, but it amused her sometimes to tease him a little.

'Is she away?'

'No.'

'I just wondered what you were doing with her dog.'

'She had to go out and couldn't take him with her, and it happens to be the housekeeper's weekend off. He could hardly be left by himself all day.'

Edmund had no intention of telling her that he and Cynthia had had a bitter and absurd quarrel that morning which had ended with her rushing from the house in a rage, he knew not where. He never discussed his wife with his mistress.

In Alys's opinion Cynthia was a stupid

bitch, but she was not herself so stupid as to say so. 'No, it simply seemed to me rather odd,' she explained, 'for someone who has always to be as careful as you do not to be recognised when you're doing anything that might be considered compromising, suddenly to appear with this large and conspicuous animal. It does seem to make rather a nonsense of our meeting with such elaborate precautions, like a couple of Russian agents, doesn't it?' She looked at him slyly. 'But perhaps it's all part of Cynthia's plan? Perhaps she's sent him to spy on us? Perhaps he's swallowed a minute tape-recorder which even now is taking down every word we say?'

Ignoring this flight of fancy, Edmund lightly remarked that Alys, being half-Argentinian, didn't understand the mystical streak in the English character which knew instinctively that anyone who loved dogs must be *all right* whatever he does. 'They wouldn't believe the evidence of their own eyes if they saw him committing murder.'

'You mean, like Bill Sikes?'

'Bill Sikes lost his head,' said Edmund, dismissing this awkward example. 'It's a principle that works very well. Other politicians would do well to bear it in mind. Chamberlain, and Wilson, to name but a few, would never have been so disliked if they had taken a dear faithful doggy as their symbol instead of a pipe — a terribly suspect object ever since Freud told us what it meant.'

'I *like* that. I shall work it into one of my answers next time I'm on the box,' said the girl, smiling. Alys was one of those curious beings who, without any special skills, had acquired a surprising fame and fortune by becoming what was called a T.V. personality. True, she had charm and intelligence, as well as the quick-wittedness essential to this odd profession. She had style, and striking good looks, with her long aristocratic face, fine expressive eyes, and a mouth that was like some rich exotic fruit. But she doubted that any of these qualities had much to do with it. Alys had never really understood how she had fallen into her success and suspected uneasily it wouldn't last when the public grew bored with seeing her.

She was a life-loving sexy girl, fond of Edmund himself as well as enjoying his love-making. There was something terribly endearing about him; he was such a kind man, and he had a way of listening to one with so much interest that, assured of his attention, one found oneself telling him all sorts of things one had thought never to have told a living soul. The great thing one felt about him was that he never judged one and it gave one an unaccustomed feeling of freedom. He would have made a marvelous priest, she had told him once, but, she had added with a sensual kiss, she was glad he was not.

The one thing she did not like was all this meeting in secrecy, though she understood it was necessary. It made her feel, she said, like a kept woman. A phrase to which she gave the novel interpretation of 'a woman who has to be kept out of sight'.

But quite apart from his bitch of a wife, a man in Edmund's position could not afford the least hint of scandal. Alys quite saw that it could wreck his entire career. And of course, though she adored Edmund, he was not the only man in her life. There was no word for 'fidelity' in her language, a fact of which Edmund was perfectly aware and, yes, he accepted it. It added a kind of spice to their relationship to know that it had so unstable a basis.

'You've become very silent, darling: what are you thinking?' Alys inquired presently.

Edmund, who had been staring through the windscreen at the near-side mirror, said: 'I think we're being followed. There's been a black Mercedes behind us ever since we left Horsham, always keeping well in the background, but I notice it never gets any nearer or makes any attempt to pass other cars.'

'If he is following us, he must be stupid and not very good at his job to let himself be noticed so easily. I thought he was your private bodyguard or something, keeping an eye on you.'

'You noticed it too. You never mentioned it.'

'I was being tactful, darling.'

'If it had been a bodyguard, he'd be keeping right behind me the whole time, never allowing another car to get between us. And in the second place, Thompson doesn't accompany me on this sort of personal expedition.'

'I ought to have realised that we've never been shadowed before, but I suppose I thought things would be different now with these Geneva talks coming up. What do you want me to do? Try to shake him off?'

'If you can, yes.'

Alys smiled. She accelerated and swung with a sudden screech of tyres off the motor-road into a tree-lined lane. They were driving through a placid English country scene with cows grazing in a field beyond the trees. The Mercedes came into view behind them. Alys put on speed and drove recklessly down one turning after another. They were almost certain they had shaken it off when it appeared again. Alys tried some fancy double-tracking. They jolted vilely up a rutted cart track that marched between the sprawling barns and byres of an ancient farm of faded red brick.

Here the road ended and she brought the car to a halt. They waited, listening for the sound of a car on the road behind them. But all that could be heard was the throbbing of an unseen tractor nearby. An adventurous piglet trotted hurriedly across the yard. Two hens padded about, pecking in the dust among the random spikes of straw. Somewhere a cow lowed mournfully for her calf.

'What depressing places farms are,' said Alys. 'I hate them.'

'Why, darling?'

'All that slaughter going on. I mean, a farm really does rub your nose in it.'

'Does the thought of death upset you?'

'Not for myself. I mean, it's something so remote as to seem unbelievable. But — Oh,' she said, looking away, 'let's not be morbid on a day like this.' She leaned forward to offer him her mouth, but at that moment the farm collie appeared, and Beau and he at once started up a vulgar shouting match.

Deafened by the operatic *basso pro-fundo* baying beside her left ear and helpless with laughter, Alys struggled to reverse the car across the deep ruts and finally succeeded.

'I think we've lost him, anyway,' she said, as they drove out into the clear. 'I wonder which of us was being followed,' she mused.

'Now, what have you been up to that someone should want to have you followed?'

Alys said vaguely: 'One never knows, does one? People get such queer ideas about one.' She glanced at the slender diamond watch on her wrist. 'Do you know, it's gone half-past one. I'm starving, aren't you?'

Edmund agreed that a nice meal would be pleasant.

'Somewhere along this road there's a rather cute little pub,' Alys recalled. And a moment later, as though she had conjured it up, there it was lying behind a bend in the road.

The dining-room was long and narrow. Each table was hidden by the sort of high-backed wooden pews typical of old chop-houses. It looked cosy and gave the diner an illusory sense of privacy. Edmund and Alys were given a table by the window, and a girl with long golden hair came to take their order. When his orders had been taken, Edmund leaned back in his corner and smiled at Alys with pleasure. He captured one slim ankle between his and raised his glass in salute.

'You're looking very lovely,' he said softly. 'Where did you acquire that delectable tan?'

'I've just come back from a visit to your part of the world. And oddly enough, that's what I wanted to see you about.'

'My part of the world? You can't mean the chilly Cotswolds!'

'Don't be silly, of course not.' She fell silent as the smoked trout was placed before them and their glasses refilled. It was at the precise moment of this distraction that a swarthy young man entered the dining-room and chose to sit directly behind their table, back to back, as it were, with Edmund. Alys's attention was taken up with watching the activities

17

of the waiter dressing the salad, and the newcomer passed without a glance from her. He was, like Alys, in his mid-twenties. Dark glasses gave his arrogant face a look of menace. He might have been handsome if his face had not been marred with the coarse pits of old smallpox scars. He leaned back dreamily against the panelled oak division and gazed out of the window.

Alys was saying: 'I'm talking of the Middle East, darling. Jordan and Lebanon.'

Edmund frowned. 'Rather an odd place to go just now, I should have thought. Did you enjoy yourself?'

'It was fascinating. I'd never been to that part of the world before. War or no war, I wasn't going to pass up the chance when a friend who was going there on business asked me if I'd like to come along. It was a piece of great good luck for me, because he had the 'in' everywhere, and we met all sorts of people. I really felt I understood what was going on. Of course a lot of the conversation had to be through interpreters, but most of the people we talked to spoke English.'

'Are you telling me you were present at business discussions with Arabs?' Edmund said on a note of incredulity.

'Oh, not that sort of business, darling. Political business. Douglas is a political journalist. *Naturally* I wasn't there when he was interviewing the men he'd come to see. But I met a great many of them afterwards socially, in their homes, with their wives.'

'Douglas? Would that be Douglas McMurdo?'

'Darling, you are clever! Fancy you knowing him. Douglas would be surprised.'

'I know of him. He's pro-Arab and pro-terrorist. What are you doing getting mixed up with a chap like that? He's not the kind of person you should know.'

The golden-haired waitress drifted by to take the order from the table beyond.

With a rather touching naivety, Alys tried to explain Douglas's peculiar political temperament. 'He's not pro-Arab because he's anti-Jewish, but because he's anti-English, you see.'

'I'm sorry, I don't.'

'Oh, he's one of those boring old Scottish nationalists, and so he's all for small deprived minorities getting their rights.'

Edmund remarked drily that he would hardly have thought the Arab states could come under the heading of 'minorities'.

'You know perfectly well what I mean; I'm talking about the Palestinians, Edmund. Poor Douglas takes it all so to heart. It really burns him up. He's a very serious person all for lost causes and so on. A great old romantic.' She gave him a roguish smile. 'He wants to marry me.'

'I didn't know you were free,' said Edmund.

'I'm not,' the girl said, her fingers straying to the black onyx crucifix hanging from her neck inlaid with its thin gothic Christ in silver. 'I said he *wants* to marry me, not that he could.'

'Tell me, does he know about us?'

'Of course not. Is it likely that I'd speak of you to him?'

'I can't see why not: you mentioned him to me.'

'That's different. He disapproves of you.'

'Well, I reciprocate his sentiments.'

Alys paused while the waiter helped her to a portion of strawberry flan. When he had served Edmund, she said:

'In a funny sort of way, you owe him something. If it weren't for him, I mightn't be here with you. I mean, if he hadn't taken me to Amman, I would never have heard the PFLP discussing ways and means of getting rid of you. This is why I said I had to see you. Darling, I'm sure you don't realise the danger you're in.' She lowered her voice. 'They *hate* you, Edmund. They're afraid you'll succeed in puffing off these peace talks, I suppose.'

'Well, that's encouraging.'

'Please don't make jokes; it's nothing to laugh at. They're terrorists.'

'Who's laughing, my dear? I simply find it rather cheering to know they take me so seriously. It gives one hope, in a curious way.'

'Douglas says they mean to stop you going to the peace talks, and if the only way to do it is to kill you, then they'll kill you. Without the least hesitation.'

'I know that too. There's nothing new about it. My life has been threatened by one group or another ever since I took on this job.'

'Only, these people mean it.'

'That doesn't mean they'll succeed. It's awfully sweet of you to tell me, but you mustn't worry about it.'

'Please don't be so stupid, Edmund!' she snapped. 'Can't you understand that I was *there*, I *heard* them: they were talking about it to Douglas quite openly.'

She remembered that evening very well. She had made Douglas take her along, thinking it would be fun. In fact it had been boring, everybody heatedly discussing the war as usual. The conversation had been mainly in Arabic, which made it worse. But then she had caught Edmund's name; they were tossing it from one to another like a ball. She had asked Douglas what they were saying. What she could not bring herself to tell

Edmund was that Douglas had been advising and encouraging them. She said:

'Surely you know what they're like. People are being killed by them every day of the week, taken hostage or shot down in cold blood or blown to smithereens with equal indifference. You can't think they'd hesitate to put you out of the way too?' She glanced vaguely at the man from the next table as he passed.

The other people had long since gone; they were the only ones left. 'Shall we go?' Edmund said, and signalled to the waiter. 'Let's not talk about it anymore,' he said winningly, putting his hand over hers when the waiter had gone. 'It's boring.'

She turned her warm velvety eyes to him with an expression of tender reproach. 'I only want to know what you're going to do about it, darling,' she murmured.

'There's nothing I can do, my dear. The risk goes with the job and one just accepts it. It would be impossible to undertake a job of this kind if one were to be forever looking over one's shoulder for the bogeyman.'

They walked out into the sunshine.

'You could resign,' she said gravely.

'Not on your life, my sweet girl. This is the biggest thing I've ever had, and I wouldn't drop it for the world. It's not a question of personal ambition; it's much more important to me than my own little life. If I can get the Arabs and Israelis to agree terms and prevent this wretched conflict escalating into a third major war, I shall really have done something and given this funny old world a chance to live in peace. I'd rather do that than save my skin, ducky. I'm sure you can understand that.'

'I do hate people being brave,' she sighed.

'Oh, Alys, don't be silly. I'm not at all keen to be assassinated and even less keen to have perfectly innocent bystanders injured and perhaps killed at the same time. I don't like that one bit. But these friends of yours are fanatics, and fanatics are not susceptible to reason.' He clasped her slim neck under its warm fall of hair. 'Oh dear, what a terrible lot of time we've wasted talking. Need we waste any more?'

24

'Do you want to come back to the flat?'

'Unwise. Isn't there a nice quiet spot somewhere round here where poor old Bobo could have some exercise too? He's been awfully good.'

'We'll go up to Torrington Common. There's not likely to be anyone there at this time of day. But you'll have to take Bobo by yourself; these sandals aren't made for country walks,' she said, lifting up the thin high-heeled soles with their delicate straps.

'We'll see, we'll see,' Edmund said. And she started up the engine.

From a narrow tree-shaded spot further down, the dark young man from the restaurant watched them pass. He gave them time to get out of sight before he began to follow in the black Mercedes.

2

Edmund was horribly late. It was a question in his mind whether he would not be too late for his scheduled spot in *World Scene*. It had suddenly become a matter of some importance to him to appear in it, and what aroused his anxiety was that he simply had first to go and change into a sober lounge suit, as befitted the discussion of a serious subject.

He and his wife had a charming Georgian house in Arundel Place in the Borough of Westminster, within ten minutes' walk of the House, which made it very convenient for Edmund. Edmund was across the pavement and up the steps almost before his car door had slammed to. He ran upstairs, without pausing to look for messages or pick up letters from the hall table, unbuttoning his shirt as he went. Halfway up, he was halted by a woman's voice calling to him from below.

He glanced over the curving bronze balustrade. His wife was gazing up at him from the drawing-room doorway with that look, which once had had such a devastating effect upon him, of a frail and wistful child. It still did something to him, though he knew now that she was really as tough as an old boot.

'Hullo,' he said. 'Didn't expect to find you here. Pleasant surprise.'

Cynthia said plaintively: 'Edmund, please don't be disagreeable. I've had a wretched day. I know I said some beastly things, but it really was as much your fault.'

'I didn't mean to sound disagreeable; I'm delighted to see you. Forgive me, my dear, but I'm going to be late . . . if I don't hurry . . . ' He took the turn in the stairs two at a time and vanished from sight.

'Where's Beau?' she called after him. But he didn't hear. Or chose not to answer. That was always the way it was now: never any time to talk. If ever they were alone together, their conversation seemed artificial. It was like meringue

— brittle, tasteless, unsubstantial and unsatisfying. Or they quarreled.

Cynthia had been thinking about it all day, knowing how much she herself was to blame for its decline, and vowing she would do her best not to give cause again. But now the familiar sense of exasperation swept over her, and she rushed after him up the stairs. She burst in on him as he was removing his trousers and demanded in an accusing tone to know where Beau was.

Oh God, this is it! he thought. He said, gently, 'I don't know, Cinzia,' pronouncing her name in the Italian way — which sounded like *Chintsia* — and which he alone used. 'I'm sorry, darling.'

'What d'you mean?'

Edmund pulled a clean shirt over his head. 'I lost him. He ran away.' He plucked a tie from the rack. 'I called and searched everywhere. But I couldn't find him, and eventually I had to give up.'

'You just left him!'

'It would be more accurate to say he left me.'

'You abandoned him, then. A puppy

hardly more than a year old.'

'As a matter of fact,' said Edmund, tucking in his shirt, 'you were the one who abandoned him. That was why I had to take him with me — at some personal inconvenience.'

'Oh, how typical! You can't even admit you behaved like a skunk,' she raged.

'I behaved like a skunk. Is anything to be gained by slanging me? It was an accident. You know I wouldn't have had it happen for the world.'

His wife turned away, tears frosting her lashes. 'Where did you lose him?'

He reached into the wardrobe for his jacket. 'I took him into Hyde Park for a run and he slipped his lead and made off. He'll come back, don't worry. He's got our phone number on his collar.'

'He happens to be a very valuable dog. What makes you so sure whoever finds him won't keep him?'

'Because, my dear girl, I've offered a fifty-pound reward. Do stop fussing; I've seen to everything. I reported his loss to the police and gave them his description and our address, and they promised to look out for him.' He pecked her on the temple as he passed. 'Simply must go now, I'm sorry.'

She followed him down the stairs.

'I'm out to dinner tonight. But Mrs. R. will have left something in the fridge if you want it; it'll only need heating.'

'All right.'

'You haven't forgotten we're invited this evening to the American Embassy for drinks?'

Edmund made a little face. 'Want me to pick you up on my way back?'

'I don't think I'll bother, if you're putting in an appearance. Make my excuses, will you? Say I've got a headache — which is the truth.'

He nodded and was gone.

★　★　★

Staring gravely straight into the lens of the No. 1 camera, the redoubtable Reg Brandywine turned from a discussion of a bank strike threatening the Big Five to remark that today, barely forty hours before the Geneva peace talks were due to begin, it had been learned that Soviet Russia had delivered to President Sadat her new long-range guided missile. This, Mr. Brandywine informed his listeners, was probably the most serious move that had yet been made in the entire Arab-Israeli conflict. The secretary of state for Mediterranean affairs, on the eve of his departure for Geneva, had come to the studio to explain to *World Scene* viewers the possible eventualities which might develop from this new move in the dangerous game of world politics. With his best profile to the camera, Mr. Brandywine declared in a properly portentous tone:

'The Right Honourable Edmund Burke!'

Camera 2 picked up Edmund looking tired and serious. Reg Brandywine's keen, fleshy, intelligent face leaned towards the secretary of state and suggested that this unexpected development must surely render any chance of the peace talks reaching a successful conclusion highly unlikely.

Edmund said that in the first place it could not be regarded as a wholly unexpected development. 'Since Soviet Russia had the missile, there was always the possibility that she would sell it to Egypt. The danger is, of course, that it might lead to an escalation of the present localised conflict. That is, if the Israelis don't manage to destroy the missiles first; and the Arabs learn to use them efficiently.'

'You don't then regard it as a very serious matter?'

'Oh yes I do. Serious, but not hopeless.'

'Do you think Russia timed this move with the intention of wrecking the peace talks, or is it only an unlucky coincidence?'

Edmund gave a half smile. 'It would be nice to think it was deliberate, because that would mean they believed the talks might be successful, which would be very cheering.'

'Do you then think the talks will not be successful, Mr. Burke?'

'On the contrary. I am very sanguine about the results. Now more than ever. The United Arab Republics are now faced with the terror of Scylla on the one hand and the disaster of Charybdis on the other. I think they're beginning to realise to what extent they've mortgaged their future to Russia, and the prospect can hardly be pleasant for them. If terms are offered them now to which they could agree without loss of face, I think they might well snatch at the chance.'

'Really?' said Reg Brandywine on a note of incredulity. 'You believe they'd be prepared to draw out now, at the very moment when their chances of defeating the Israelis must seem better than ever before?'

Edmund conceded that the outcome of the talks must ultimately depend on the sincerity and goodwill of those participating, and the degree to which they were willing and able to set aside old grievances and prejudices. If either side or both came looking first and foremost for the acceptance of their own demands, then it was unlikely that any further advance would be arrived at. But if they came with the determination to give in order to reach a settlement, then there was no reason why agreement should not be reached in good faith. In fact, just because the situation was so critical, Edmund thought it was more hopeful.

Brandywine mentioned an idea that had been broached for a five-mile-wider border between the U.A.R. and Israel, to be manned by a neutral NATO force to maintain peace. How did the secretary of state for Mediterranean affairs regard that proposition? Edmund replied that it was not his idea of peace.

'You wouldn't propose it as a solution?'

'It's not my brief to produce a solution for them to agree to; my job is to help them find their own solution. I'm not taking any ready-made proposals from the four powers with me to Geneva. Nor are the antagonists going to have to sit facing one another round a table. In my opinion that's asking for trouble, all the rage and bitterness coming to the fore. We believe we stand a better chance of success with the Rhodes formula devised by Dr. Bunche in 1948, whereby the parties are not invited to meet until the proposals have been discussed privately, with in this case myself acting as intermediary. My task is simply that of a go-between, to see if some measure of agreement can be reached at the lowest common denominator. It doesn't matter how simple and trivial it may be; that first subject for agreement will be a foundation from which to work up to the greater and graver issues.'

'You'll have to be something rather more than a go-between to arrive at a peace settlement, I would think,' Brandywine said with a dry smile.

'I'm not pretending it can all be done at once.'

'You're an optimist, Mr. Burke.'

'If an optimist is someone who believes that every problem has a solution, then I am an optimist.'

'You think the problem of the Palestinians is also able to be solved?'

'Given goodwill on both sides.'

'I mean, if an agreement is reached by the U.A.R. and Israel, do you suppose the PFLP will simply subside? Do you think that will really be the end of the trouble? That there will be no more acts of terrorism, no more skyjacking?'

'That's not within my brief; it's a matter for the U.A.R.'

'And if PFLP and El F'tah and the other commando organisations join together to overthrow their heads of state and seize power for themselves, where will your peace be then? And isn't that the real issue, Mr. Burke? Is any peace to be secured which ignores the demands of the Palestinian terrorists?'

Edmund sat up straighter and opened his mouth to reply, but before he had uttered half a sentence, Brandywine, with an apologetic smile but an ill-concealed glint of triumph in his eye, said he was afraid they had run out of time and they had to stop there.

'Mr. Burke,' he said — and there was a flourish of trumpets in his voice, 'Thank you very much.'

The camera had the last word, with its final shot of the secretary of state for Mediterranean affairs sinking back in his seat with an air of exasperation on his usually good-humoured face.

★　★　★

From the television centre, Edmund drove to the embassy in Grosvenor Square. The ambassador gave these informal parties once or twice a month. It was not strictly necessary for Edmund to put in an appearance, but particularly now he wanted people to remember having seen him, should occasion arise in the future.

Edmund found his hostess, remarked how very nice it was to see her again, and began to apologise for Cynthia's unavoidable absence, which she greatly regretted — at which point the ambassador's wife broke in to say:

'Why, Mr. Burke, your lovely wife is here! I said hello to her not ten minutes ago. She came with Lord Nevinson.'

'I wish there were some way of computerising women, the incalculable sex,' Edmund commented with a tolerant smile.

'It'll come, Mr. Burke, I have no doubt it'll come. And then how dull you men will be.'

As he helped himself to a martini, Edmund was nobbled by a Pennsylvanian industrialist he had met once before. With an attentive expression, Edmund let the stream of statistics bore into his ear in a monotonous drone. There was no need to speak; he had only to nod from time to time. He raised a hand in greeting to the first familiar face that passed and excused himself to the Pennsylvanian Niagara.

Chatting a few minutes with this one and that one, Edmund gradually made his way into the salon through the arch. He saw Cynthia standing by the gladioli-filled fireplace with a tall gentleman in horn-rimmed glasses on either side of her. The men were laughing, and from the innocent expression on her face, he guessed she had just made one of her shattering remarks.

The young thin fair man, Edmund recognised as one of the American attachés. The other was Lord Nevinson, a recently created press baron. He was a heavily built man, not particularly good-looking. Yet he had one invincible attraction — he was a multi-millionaire.

In a materialistic world, it is inevitable that the man with the most money is king. King Midas rules again. Only now, nobody whispers that under his crown he has ass's ears, because all that matters is that he has the mysterious power to turn everything he touches into gold.

The story went that Mark Nevinson had gone to Canada at the age of sixteen, and was said to have worked his way up from lumberjack in the timber forests to owning at the age of twenty-six a small-town newspaper, the first of many. Now he owned two English national papers, a Sunday and a daily, and also a political weekly. One could say he had fairly good control of the current scene.

He was at that moment elucidating admirably to the young attaché the precise difference over union procedure in the dockers' strike currently paralysing the Port of London and the earlier waterfront strikes of the New York longshoremen, when Edmund joined them. Cynthia was watching Nevinson as though the subject fascinated her.

Edmund nodded cordially to Nevinson, whom he did not like, and laid a caressing hand on his wife's shoulder. He said pleasantly, as the attache faded discreetly away, 'Now, how did you manage to persuade her to come along, Nevinson? She wouldn't for me.'

In his agreeable Canadian accent, Lord Nevinson replied: 'I'm not her husband; I guess that gives me a kind of advantage.'

'You consider it's an advantage not to be her husband?'

Lord Nevinson laughed. 'I won't have that; you're putting words into my mouth. You politicians are as bad as attorneys.'

'I should stand on the Fifth Amendment, Mark, on the grounds that to answer might incriminate you,' Cynthia offered.

Nevinson smiled at her with the kind of glance one gives an adorable child who has said something cute but must not be openly admired. He was so much in love with her that he was quite unable to conceal it even from her husband.

The urbane Mr. Burke was surprised by a twinge of rage, as though some atavistic ancestor had suddenly taken possession of him. He would have liked at that moment to kick all Nevinson's smiling teeth down his throat, and wondered at his uncivilised reaction.

He knew they were lovers. Knew Mark wanted to marry her. It would be absurd to pretend he was still in love with her himself in the authentic obsessive way Mark was. Once upon a time he had been, when he had first succeeded in capturing 'Society's No. 1. deb, the lovely Cynthia Bedford', as the glossies had described her at the time. He had been crazy about her for the first five years or so of their marriage. That might be over, but she was still his wife, and she represented something more to him than physical passion. They had only one child, a boy, who next year would be going to Eton. He loved the boy and was proud of him. It was not Edmund's nature to be a dog-in-the-manger. If it had not meant ruining his own life, he would have let her go. But he had been married thirteen years, and he did not see himself allowing this well-built social structure to be broken up without resistance.

Nevinson had been married twice (a modest enough tally for a millionaire), and both his wives had died: one of cancer, the other in a motor crash. He had loved each of them deeply. Yet it was in a way lucky for him they had died. For if Shirley had not died, he could never have married Betty, and if Betty in her turn had not been killed, heaven alone knew how he would have dealt with his passion for Cynthia. He would not have been able to free himself from Betty because he did not believe in divorce. Divorce had been forbidden by the Lord Jesus Christ. So he had been taught, and this quaint old-fashioned tenet was left rooted in him like the fang of a tooth by his stern Presbyterian upbringing. The trouble with people of limited religious sensibilities was that they tended to remain unquestioningly under the powerful but misapprehended influences of teachings they absorbed at their mother's knee. It might on the face of it sound incredible that a sophisticated newspaperman of considerable business acumen and great wealth should be dominated by what he had been taught nearly forty years earlier, but that was the way it was.

He was a greedy man, Mark Nevinson. He wanted jam with it. In other words, he wanted Edmund not only to agree to a divorce, but to agree to Cynthia divorcing him. Millionaires tended to think they could always get their own way. And unfortunately they usually could, which gradually gave them the idea that they had a right to it.

But as Edmund said reasonably enough to Cynthia, 'Why should I? You're my wife; I don't want to divorce you, much less allow you to divorce me.' To which she had replied that she did not see how he could stop her.

'You have to have grounds,' he pointed out.

'That shouldn't be difficult,' she had retorted with a crooked smile.

After which exchange, Edmund had taken care to be exceptionally discreet in his private life. A cabinet minister was singularly vulnerable.

At this particular moment in his life, a scandal could jeopardise much more than his own career. Edmund therefore had urged Cynthia to wait for a more prudent moment in which to sue for divorce. In the special circumstances, it seemed to him little enough to ask. But Cynthia wanted Mark, and perhaps somewhere deep down was afraid of losing him if she could not encircle him quickly with a wedding ring. Mark was a man of very strong feelings, and even stronger will. Edmund did not trust him. The alternative was for Edmund to get in first, divorcing Cynthia for adultery and citing Nevinson as co-respondent.

Cynthia had wrung her hands at this, declaring it would ruin everything. She tried to explain to her husband Mark's strong and irrational feelings about marriage and divorce. To be the co-respondent in a divorce suit would undermine his own peculiar idea of self-respect. He would feel himself to be publicly defiled. And, worse still in his eyes, Cynthia would be defiled too. It was impossible, absolutely out of the question. She had to implore Edmund not to contemplate such a move.

There were besides, Cynthia considered, her own feelings in the matter to be taken into account. She might be prepared to destroy thirteen years of modestly happy marriage, but she was not prepared to forego her natural claim on the boy. If she were the guilty party, some stupid judge might consider that since Nicholas was in his teens, he had more need of his father than his mother, and so would refuse her the custody of her own son, granting her only limited access to him instead. The notion was not to be borne. She would never consent to it. Cynthia considered that it should be perfectly obvious to any rational human being that the child belonged to the mother.

So for the time being there they all were, caught in a queer kind of cat's cradle.

3

On quitting the embassy, Edmund made for Rotherhithe, to what once had been an old warehouse overhanging the river. The entrance was at the side of the building, up a flight of dilapidated wooden steps.

Edmund thumped the heavy iron knocker three times, and waited. From somewhere higher up the river, he could hear a foghorn's melancholy hoot. Lights shone through the rising mist like blurred moons, wan and vague.

He was on the point of turning away in despair when the door opened. Against a dimly lit background, a dark figure blocked the entrance. It said harshly: 'I'm busy. Go away and come back tomorrow,' and with this admonition the door closed.

Before the door shut quite, Edmund said loudly and emphatically: 'But it's now that I want to see you, Percival.'

The door flew wide. 'Edmund! Is it

really you? My dear fellow!' A hand grasped his and pulled him in. 'How good to see you, old friend! What brings you to these regions?'

'I happened to be down this way and I thought I'd come by and see if you were still in England.'

'How long is it?'

'Must be nearly five years.'

Their hands fell apart.

'Is it really not convenient?'

'Nonsense, my dear chap.' A hand on Edmund's shoulder urged him forward. 'I have to chase away people who come and knock me up when they've got a skinful. I have to be pretty sharp with them.'

They were in a vast cavernous chamber illumined by a single table-lamp in the middle of the room, shedding its circle of calm light over a muddle of books and papers, half open maps, and a typewriter. Percival had simply taken one whole floor of the warehouse and made it just as it was into a useful and convenient dwelling for himself. He liked the feeling of space — an advantage singularly lacking in modern cities. He was used to immense vistas and empty skies. The only alteration he had made was to replace the wall on the river side with glass, through which could be seen the occasional lights of the river traffic gliding slowly past.

The disused warehouse was Percival's pied-a-terre, the nearest thing to a permanent residence he possessed. Edmund noticed a wide divan in one corner spread with a fur rug. A damascened dagger gleamed on the wall above it. Here and there the gilt on a book spine glinted softly in the dusk. Carpets from Bokhara and Isfahan adorned the floor. These few simple articles somehow produced an atmosphere of austere luxury, like the tent of some wealthy nomad chief. The simile was not altogether far-fetched, since Percival spent his life travelling to distant and out-of-the-way places of the earth.

Though the men met rarely, they had been friends for more than thirty years — since their schooldays. Curious really, because their lives drew them always further apart: Edmund being concerned with making civilisation work, whereas

Percival loathed the whole concept of contemporary life and truly admired only the untamed barbarous peoples of the world. Odd too, for their lives, character and temperament were utterly opposed: Edmund by nature was gregarious, genial and sympathetic, while Percival was something of a mystic and an ascetic like most explorers, a thinker and an adventurer, sensitive and ruthless in the same streak. One could say truthfully that they had nothing in common, and yet each felt of the other that here was a man to turn to if ever he were in trouble. By some strange alchemy, however much time and experience had separated them, it made no difference; they met at once on some deeper level of understanding than mere words.

Percival kicked forward an ancient black-leather porter's chair for Edmund, brought bottles and glasses from a painted cupboard from Tashkent, and plonked them down on the marble-topped refectory table he used as his desk. He poured them each a drink and then seated himself facing Edmund across the table. For a long moment they looked at one another in silence. Edmund raised his glass in a gesture of salute and drank a little of the brandy.

'Tell me,' he said with his friendly smile, 'what are you up to these days?'

'Banging out a book once more, my dear fellow, to try and make some money.'

'Things difficult with you?'

'No, no, I live easy in my unsophisticated fashion. No, I'm hoping to raise some funds for my next expedition by making a book about my last one. Haven't seen you since then, have I? I spent eighteen months in the Empty Quarter, Arabia Infelix. Of course there's Thesiger's book and Doughty's; but then everything's been done now, hasn't it?'

'It's your personal experience which makes it unique. Your books have always been first-rate.'

'Except that they don't sell very well. They'll bring them out in too-expensive editions. Whenever I walk into a London bookshop, I always seem to see remaindered copies.' A sudden thought struck him. 'Have you eaten yet?'

'No. I wasn't hungry.'

'I haven't eaten all day and suddenly I'm ravenous. Will a salami sandwich do you?'

'Where's the next expedition to be?' Edmund inquired as Percival cut hair-thin slices of the sausage and stuffed them between slices of crisp buttery bread.

'The kingdom of Hunza. It's a little wedge of a place in the middle of the Himalayas. An adorable unspoilt country where people live to be a hundred and twenty years old, subsisting mainly on a diet of apricots.'

Edmund murmured that it sounded fascinating, like Shangri-la.

'It's been a dream of mine for years, and I'm beginning to feel that if I don't buck up, I shall soon be too old to undertake such an arduous journey. Really, it's now or never. The problem is finding the money.'

'It's going to be very costly?'

'Oh, enormously. Planes to charter, jeeps to buy and so on. I was thinking of hiring myself out as a guide to some rich

Americans, only it *would* spoil the fun, wouldn't it?'

'You mustn't consider it, Percival. God, I wish I could go with you!' Edmund muttered in heartfelt tones.

'I wish you could.'

'How much longer will it take you to finish this book?'

'Four or five months, say.'

'And how much do you reckon to make out of it?'

Percival shrugged. 'Five or six hundred perhaps. Maybe a thousand if I'm lucky and it catches the public interest, and the publisher doesn't cost it at more than seventy shillings retail.'

'But a thousand won't be enough, will it? You'll need twice that at least, surely.'

'Oh, I'll manage,' Percival said. 'I might be able to get a soup company or something to pay for some advertising.'

Edmund said softly, 'Tell me how much you want. I'll back you. I'll finance the expedition for you. Let me, Percival — I'd like to.'

Percival's face broke into a smile. 'You old madman! Thanks all the same.'

The initial refusal was followed by expostulation and protest, then came a brief argument, which gradually dissolved into a lengthy discussion of all the necessities for the month-long journey, the stores, the equipment, the hiring of experienced guides, the plane to fly one into the heart of the Himalayas, and so on and so on. To all of which Edmund listened with attention and sympathy — as if he had nothing else on his mind.

'Dear God, I can hardly believe it,' Percival murmured at last. 'It means I'm free to go as soon as I'm fitted up. You've saved my life, Edmund. I don't know how I can ever repay you.'

There was an odd pause. And then Edmund said: 'Save mine.'

Percival gazed at him for a long moment. 'Is something wrong, Ned?'

'Very.' He raised the glass to his lips to conceal their trembling.

Percival suddenly noticed that Edmund's face was pale in the lamplight, and it gave him the idea that Edmund was ill, perhaps smitten with some dread disease, and it flashed through his mind that Ned was going to ask him to be a guardian to the boy Nicholas,. 'You know,' he said, 'I'll do anything I can.'

'I know.' He fell silent again.

Percival said: 'I imagine you don't want Cynthia to know.'

'Cynthia?' Edmund said, surprised, and he looked as if he had inadvertently swallowed something bitter. 'No, it wouldn't do for Cynthia to know.' He went over to the glass wall and stared out at the water slipping by. The early evening mist had dissipated and the murky reddish glow of the London night sky was reflected brokenly in the water. In little more than an hour it would be dark. Edmund closed his eyes and leaned his forehead on the cool glass, battling against a feeling of immense weariness which threatened to overwhelm him. 'God help me!' he said silently to the God in whose existence he did not believe.

Percival, sitting quietly waiting, said: 'What's the trouble?'

'I'm in the most frightful bloody mess.

I don't know whether I have the right to involve you.'

'Don't be absurd!'

'You don't know what it's about yet. The fact is, it's a criminal matter. If I confide in you, it makes you an accessory.'

Percival laughed. 'Are you talking to me, the old gun-runner for Ojukwu, me the ex-colonel of the Congo mercenaries? Come off it, Ned! Since when have I troubled my head about society's arbitrary rules?'

Edmund came slowly back to his chair and sank into it. 'It is hard to be a politician and an ordinary sensual man, Percival. Politicians are expected to be above reproach. The people whose interests we represent expect of us standards they do not themselves keep. They make us into hypocrites, pretending to a virtue we don't possess. It's part of the stupid game the political set-up obliges us to play. Yet if we're serious in our wish to serve our country, there's nothing else we can do. I play the game as best I can, and when I'm having an affair I try to be reasonably discreet. There hasn't been anyone serious for a long time now. But about two years ago, I met a girl.' He paused and reached out for his glass and sipped at it thoughtfully. 'She was a charming, beautiful, intelligent creature, and I was very fond of her. We both enjoyed our relationship, such as it was. There was nothing permanent about it; it was casual, friendly and delightful. Like most girls today, she believed in sexual freedom. And why not?' He glanced towards the darkening scene outside.

'But all that ceased when I became a privy councillor and was offered the job of trying to bring about a solution to the Arab-Israeli conflict. That meant a great deal to me. It was my big opportunity to achieve something really worthwhile. It gave me little time for my private life, and besides, I needed to be especially careful; I couldn't afford to take risks which might wreck my career. We stopped meeting.

'And then this morning she phoned me. She'd never done such a thing before. She said she had to see me; that it was important. There were a hundred and one things to be done before I leave for Geneva tomorrow, and it really seemed impossible for me to get away. I asked her if she couldn't write it, and she said no, she couldn't, it was something I must know about before I left.' Edmund shrugged ruefully. 'So I went. Martin, my secretary, was to cover up for me if necessary.' He rose and siphoned some soda into his glass and drank it thirstily.

'We arranged to meet halfway, in Horsham. I left my car there and she picked me up. I was somehow on edge all the while, and the fidgety feeling was not lessened by the gradual conviction that we were being followed. However, she was a skilful driver and she managed to shake him off. We had lunch at a country pub and then drove into a little copse on the edge of a broad heath. I wanted to take the dog for a run — did I say I had had to bring our dog with me? Anyway, Alys had on some absurdly fragile footwear in which no one could possibly walk on that rough ground. So we sat in the car till the poor dog became restless and began to whimper, and presently I opened the door and let him out. I never dreamed he'd go off by himself. But he did.' Edmund gazed into space. 'I suppose if he hadn't, none of this would have happened. It's a dreadful thought.' He rubbed the back of his hand against his brow as though it ached. His eyes, Percival noticed, were ringed with shadow.

'When I got out of the car, he was nowhere to be seen. I called and whistled but he never came back. I searched the heath from end to end. I dreaded having to return home without him; Cynthia doted on that animal. But I had to give up in the end. When I got back to the car,' Edmund said, staring fixedly at Percival but as though he didn't know he was there, 'Alys was leaning against the open window frame, her head on her breast. I thought she was asleep, until I touched her and found that she was dead.'

Percival frowned. 'So suddenly?'

'It's the sort of thing one can hardly believe. I was really petrified with horror.

At first it was for her, and then gradually it turned into horror for myself at the predicament it had put me in.'

'How do you mean?'

'I must sound incredible and disgusting that I should be thinking of myself at such a time. But *she* was dead; nothing mattered to her anymore. Whereas I . . . I had to decide what to do. Every moment that passed made it worse. I felt as though Time was a great wheel advancing with increasing rapidity to crush me,' he said with a graphic gesture.

'I don't understand.'

'Don't you? The girl was dead. I ought to have sent for a doctor, obviously. If I did, he would call in the police, he would have to. The girl had clearly been murdered.'

'Murdered!' interjected Percival. 'How?'

'I don't know. Strangled, perhaps. Or stabbed with some instrument too fine to leave a mark.'

'Christ! Who could have done it? And why?'

'How can I tell? It may have been someone she knew who stopped to speak to her, someone she would have faced without fear. Or maybe someone stopped ostensibly to ask the way. There was no sign that I could find of anyone having been there. Which only made it the worse for me. I was the one who had been with her, the one who had found her dead. Was anyone going to believe that I had left her alone for half an hour or so and when I came back she was dead? Is it likely, I ask you! Do you see now what a frightful position it put me in? It's easy to say I ought to have gone for the police or fetched a doctor. But I could visualise only too vividly what would happen if I did.' He began to pace the room.

'I suppose the police might not have stopped me going to Geneva tomorrow, since I am after all one of her majesty's privy councilors. But I'd certainly be their chief suspect. And there was the question of the press. Once *they* got hold of the story, all hell would break over my head. They'd crucify me. I tell you frankly, Percival, I couldn't face it. Not because it would mean the ruin of my career. I wasn't thinking of my private life or my personal ambitions, I swear. I was thinking only of what would happen in the Middle East if I was to be kicked out of the government at this particularly crucial moment. And I was weighing all this in the balance against the murder of one girl — a girl of whom I happened to be very fond. One girl's death against the unnumbered thousands of future dead if the conflict in the Middle East is allowed to perpetuate itself and spread . . . ' He drew a hand over his face in a weary gesture. 'I asked myself, Percival, what *is* justice? Alys is dead. What difference will it make to her if her murderer is caught and imprisoned for a term of years? What difference will it make to her if her death remains unavenged? Do you think I was wrong?' he asked.

'You made the decision you had to make, Edmund. But why was she killed?'

'God knows! Why *are* people murdered?'

'In the case of women, the cause can usually be summed up under one of the R's. Rape, robbery, sexual rage, or riddance.'

Edmund turned his face away. 'Don't be so bloody ghoulish.'

'I'm not. I think we should try to understand what happened. It might be important.'

'It can't have been rape,' Edmund said stiffly. 'And it wasn't robbery, because her diamond watch was still on her wrist and there was more than twenty pounds in her handbag; I looked. The only thing that was missing, as far as I could tell, was a rather beautiful onyx cross she wore inlaid with silver on a platinum chain. It can't have been as valuable as all that, surely. Hardly worth killing for. As for the rest, I don't know. I shouldn't have thought anyone would need to *rid* themselves of a girl like Alys; she wasn't the clinging type.' A thought struck him. 'Unless it was her husband, Daneforth.'

'She was married, then?' said Percival in some surprise.

'Married and separated. I can't remember whether he was a Catholic too. But Alys was, and I know they weren't divorced. I've no idea what sort of chap her husband was, except that he couldn't make a go of it with a sweet girl like Alys. Maybe he did want to rid himself of her in order to marry again. But to me it seems a far-fetched idea. And if it wasn't him, I think it must have been a stranger who killed her perhaps on impulse.'

'A pathological killer. You mean she was killed only because she happened to be in that place at the particular time the killer was there, and it might as well have been anyone?'

'I think it's probable.'

'Then if he's left free, he may kill again. Is it right to let that happen, Ned?'

'Of course it isn't *right*. I might ask, Is it right to let two nations go on slaughtering one another, or isn't it *right* for me to put a stop to it if I can? Isn't it *right* for me to put the major consideration before the lesser one? Tell me!'

'Dear old friend, I'm not criticising your judgement,' said the other mildly. 'I'm trying to follow what happened, that's all. I mean, for instance, couldn't you have rung the police without giving your name and told them there was a dead woman in a car at this particular woodland spot?'

'It did occur to me. But, you see, I needed her car in order to get back to Horsham and pick up my own car. To have taken her car and left her behind would have been already tampering with the evidence. It has to be all or nothing; one can't afford to play the fool in a situation like this. If one is prepared to conceal the evidence of a crime, then for God's sake conceal it properly, so that it won't rise up later and hit you in the face.' He was pacing restlessly up and down the long room, talking rapidly, as though he was running through a piece he'd rehearsed.

'What did you do?'

'I hid her,' Edmund murmured, his back to Percival. 'I found a place, a hollow full of leaves between three giant beeches. I carried her there wrapped in the dog's rug, scooped away the leaves and laid her down, and then heaped them back over her. It was the best I could do.' He turned to look at his friend. 'I didn't intend to leave her there. It was only a temporary measure. I needed time to think, and time was what I hadn't got. In less than three hours I was due to appear on a television programme. It hardly seemed the moment not to turn up: I needed that alibi, such as it was. And even now, there are only the next few hours remaining to me in which to get something done.' He came back into the light. 'Percival, she must be decently buried. You do see that, don't you? I owe her that much.'

'You're not seriously thinking of going back there and digging a grave? You couldn't be so crazy.'

Edmund said stiffly: 'I regard it as an obligation. A debt I must pay. If she hadn't wanted to meet me today, she might still be alive.'

'What did she want to see you about? You never said.'

'Oh . . . to warn me that *my* life was in danger. There's irony for you . . . a bitter irony. She wanted to persuade me not to go to Geneva, of all things! She was afraid I might be assassinated. She'd just come back from the Middle East and had heard the PFLP discussing ways of getting rid of me, and it alarmed her. She told me all this as though I didn't already know it. Bless her kind loyal heart, she was trying to save my life; and in doing so she lost her own. The least I can do is to give her a quiet resting place.' He gave a great sigh.

'Well, it's to protect myself too, I admit. My idea is to remove her to someplace as far away as is practicable from where the crime was committed. Just in case the body should be found at some time, or a search should be mounted for her; it would be as well for it to appear as though the crime was committed a long way from Sussex. Not that I think there's much likelihood of a search being made. I don't suppose her husband will bother, and there's no one else to make a fuss. Her mother's dead and her father lives in South America. She told me once she hadn't heard from him for years. And the BBC aren't likely to notice her absence till they want her again in the autumn. My guess is she'll be thought to have quietly disappeared and soon she'll be forgotten. It's a melancholy thought that I alone will remember her.' He sank down onto the divan. 'God, I'm weary!' he said. 'Do you think I could have a cup of black coffee?'

'How about another brandy?' Percival said, rising.

'No. I can't afford to take any chances; I've got a lot of driving to do.'

'Where do you have in mind to take her?' asked the other, casting a handful of beans into the grinder.

'Deep into the New Forest,' he murmured, falling back on the cushions and closing his eyes. 'Just five minutes,' he mumbled, and sank into slumber.

Percival regarded him meditatively. He wondered coolly whether Edmund had told him the truth, the whole truth. Not that it made any difference as far as he was concerned. He believed in Edmund (which was not the same thing as believing him). Politically speaking, Edmund was a great man. It was important that he should be allowed to play his role. As Edmund had said, what did one dead girl matter against the scene of world history? Edmund was right, he had had to do what he did. He was going to need help. Well, one did not let down a friend, and the bargain had already been struck.

4

Douglas McMurdo came out of the cinema before the film ended. The film had not done anything for him; all the way through, he had thought of Alys with a kind of restless chagrin. He left, wanting another drink before the pubs closed.

He was angry and depressed. The arrangement had been, or so McMurdo understood, that he should come down to Brighton and spend the weekend with his girl, Alys. He hadn't had time to see her since their return from Jordan, and he'd been looking forward to it. He relished the thought of the long peaceful Sunday morning in bed together, reading the papers and making love. He was naïve enough to imagine that was how it would always be if they were married.

The weekly for which he wrote came out on Friday, which meant he had the weekends free, unless he was covering a special feature. He had only to write his jazz column for Nevinson's *Sunday Edition*, and that he had knocked off this morning and dropped into the office on his way down to the coast.

He had arrived at Corunna Court in nice time for a drink or two and an enormous embrace before they went out to dinner. It had been a cracking disappointment to find Alys not there. He had gone up to her flat to see if she had by any chance left a message for him. But there was nothing.

He had waited around for a bit, helped himself to a drink, and then scrawled a message on a paper carrier-bag to say that he'd be waiting for her at the Ship Hotel. He buzzed down to it in his car and sat staring out at the Promenade, with its gay and grotesque people strutting up and down against the backcloth of a sharp greeny-grey sea. Every half hour or so, he rang the flat. But there was never any answer. At nine o'clock, having had too much to drink and not enough to eat, he had gone to the cinema.

It was past eleven when he got back to the flat and still she had not returned.

Her car was not in the forecourt or in its garage, which was open and still vacant. McMurdo couldn't imagine where she could be, and he tried not to imagine where she might be. He was suddenly aware that he was desperately in love with her. He became obsessed with the notion that for her it was the end of their affair, that her interest in him had lapsed. He could think of no other valid explanation. Poor McMurdo.

He moved restlessly around the flat. Pushing back the sliding doors of her wardrobe in an idle gesture, it occurred to him to wonder if he could tell what she might be wearing. As the garments stirred beneath his hand, there drifted out from them the poignantly evocative odour of the scent she used, and for a moment he crushed his face into a handful of silk.

From this moment of sentimental weakness, he stalked severely away. There was a piece of cold salmon in the fridge. McMurdo made himself a sandwich, poured a Scotch, and sat down to read yesterday's newspaper like a castaway on a desert island.

* ★ ★

The Gurneys were in bed, the whole house in darkness, when the night was rent by this terrifying scream. In his sleep, it woke in Mr. Gurney memories of the war. But Mrs. Gurney was out of bed and dragging on her dressing-gown before his eyes were open. She ran out of the room.

'Mummy! Mummy!' she could hear him shrieking, as though he was still a baby instead of quite a big boy — though small for his age.

She switched on the light. Philip was sitting up in bed, his face as white as a little ghost's, his dark eyes wide with terror. He clutched at her, sobbing.

'It's all right, darling, Mummy's here. You had a bad dream.'

'The eyes!' he said, and hid his face in her neck.

'There, there,' she murmured, rocking him to and fro. 'It's all over now . . . Only a nasty dream . . . '

'I'm scared,' he moaned. 'Don't leave me!'

'I'm not going to leave you, you old

silly. I'm only going to get you some hot milk. You can come with me, if you like. And then I'll sit with you till you fall asleep again.'

'No!' She could feel his body stiffen against the suggestion. 'I don't want to go to sleep. I'm afraid of dreaming about her.'

'Who?'

'The dead woman.' He shuddered.

'What dead woman?'

In a rapid undertone, he said: 'I saw a dead woman crouching under some trees. Her eyes were open and she looked up at me. I ran and I ran, and the eyes seemed to be behind me all the way. Mummy, are there such things as ghosts?'

'Of course not, darling. There's nothing to be frightened of, my baby. It was only a bad dream, you know. You woke Mummy up, crying out.'

His little fingers played with the narrow frill of lace edging the yoke of her nightgown. 'I'm not quite sure it was a dream. I don't think I'd been to sleep. I heard you and Dad come up to bed.' He smoothed the frill down with careful little pats. 'I nearly called out to you then,' he confessed.

She gazed with a puzzled frown at his now flushed cheeks. Something or someone had frightened him. One of those horrid comics perhaps. He was such a vulnerable nervous child, quite unlike the older two.

'Why didn't you call? We wouldn't have been cross.'

'I didn't know what to say,' Philip sighed. 'I was afraid you might think I had imagined it all . . . about . . . about, you know, the eyes,' he confided in a small voice. 'And I was afraid Daddy would be angry with me.'

'Whyever should he be?'

'Because . . . because . . . ' A door creaked, and Philip heard the soft flap-flap of slipper heels. He grasped her tightly round the neck and said urgently: 'You won't tell him, will you? Please!'

'Is all the excitement over?' inquired that personage, putting a tousled head round the door. 'Can we all go back to sleep now, do you think? It may be all right for some people to sit up half the night chatting, but your wretched father has to catch the 8.10 to town. So let's get our heads down, shall we?'

Mrs. Gurney said in a soothing tone, 'Phil is a bit upset, Harry. Why don't you sleep here and I'll take him in with me, so that you won't be disturbed.'

'Oh, come on now, Bet,' her husband said irritably. 'He's too old for that babyish stuff!'

Philip burst into tears, no longer clinging to his mother, but hunched up with his hands over his face. Elizabeth Gurney gave her husband a 'Now see what you've done!' look, and put an arm around the boy. 'Can't you see the child's not himself?' she murmured. The father sat down heavily beside the boy.

'Come on, old son,' he said, giving his bowed head a rough caress. 'What's the trouble? Tell Dad.'

Words gulped out of his sobs as though torn from his breaking heart: 'I . . . I . . . didn't — didn't . . . g-go to the s-swim-im-ming baths . . . D-daddy . . . '

'Didn't you? Well, never mind, it's not the end of the world, is it?'

Philip looked up cautiously. 'You said I *had* to go. You said everyone should know how to swim.'

'So they should.'

'But I didn't like it,' the boy wailed. 'Last time they tried to drown me. They kept throwing me in and pulling me out and throwing me in again. They were laughing.' His small face expressed the terror he had felt, splashing about in the pool like a desperate little dog, choking for air, with no way of escape from the grinning faces and outstretched hands above him.

'Who did it?'

'Some boys from the Fifth. I don't know their names,' he lied in the best tradition of school stories. 'It's because I'm small, I expect.'

'Why didn't you tell me?'

'I thought you'd be angry if I said I didn't want to go again. So I just didn't go with the others the last two times. I pretended to go. I wet my trunks in the rain-barrel when I came home.'

'That was very deceitful,' said his father, 'but we won't say any more about

76

it. I'm not cross, only sorry you didn't tell me about it before.' He smiled at his son reassuringly. 'There's one thing I don't understand though. What has all this to do with your waking us all up in the middle of the night?' Mr. Gurney was still smiling, but Philip's face had taken on a pinched look again.

His mother said quickly, 'It was a nightmare, Harry.'

'It wasn't a nightmare *really*,' Philip said. 'I hadn't been to sleep. I was too scared.' He took hold of his father's hand. 'Scared,' he said bravely, 'of what I saw in the wood this afternoon.'

His father gave him a stern glance. 'This isn't a try-on, is it, Philip?'

'No, Dad, honestly.' Philip's lower lip began to quiver.

'All right. Tell me what it was you saw that frightened you.'

Philip's story was that he'd gone up to Torrington Common to while the hours away till he was due home from the baths. He was practising catches and kicks with an old ball. Kicking it homeward through the wood, the ball had ricocheted off a tree trunk and disappeared into a little valley. Philip had jumped down after it on to a heap of fallen leaves. He had landed on something uneven, lost his balance and gone sprawling, and found himself staring into a pair of eyes beneath the leaves gazing past him up at the broken fragments of blue sky.

He felt himself going to pieces, as if he was all made of water and jelly. It was the first time in his life he had seen anyone dead. Her hair caught in his fingers as he tried to push himself upright, and the more he struggled to climb out, the more the dry old leaves rustled and fluttered and shifted, disclosing more of their secret to the horrified eyes of the boy. Bits of dark rug, bits of bare flesh, showed through the leaves. The woman seemed to be sort of hunched up on her back with her knees bent up to her stomach. It was all these hidden juttings and hollows, the bony places and the soft ones, that made it so hard for him to keep his feet. But he did scramble out at last. And then he ran, without stopping, all the way home . . .

No comfort for him even then. He could not pour out his dreadful secret, because it would mean telling that he had not gone to the baths with the rest of the boys, and his father would be angry and his mother shocked. He had kept the burden in his soul for more than six hours. But in the silence and darkness, his own private terrors became too much for him: he sat up in bed and screamed at the ghost with the terrible eyes, screamed for his mother to take it away . . .

Late though it was, Mr. Gurney at once phoned the police. He had thought merely to pass the information to them, supposing that once it was in police hands they could safely go back to their beds. But it wasn't like that at all. The duty officer had simply said he would send someone round, and rang off before Harry could protest. Ten minutes later, a police car was at the door.

Detective Inspector Yapp was a deceptively mild-mannered man with large sad eyes and a gentle smile. The sort of man one instinctively trusts. He listened to

Philip with scarcely an interruption, and at the end asked only a few questions. And then he said:

'Now, if you wouldn't mind getting a few clothes on, I'd like you and your mother and father, Philip, to come with me in the car and show me just where it was you think you saw the dead woman.'

'At this time of night!' said Mr. Gurney indignantly. 'Surely the boy has been through quite enough for one day? Why can't your policemen search for themselves? That's their job, isn't it? It's only a few hundred feet square. Not really a wood at all.'

'Because it might take hours instead of minutes to do it without help. And we haven't the men to spare, Mr. Gurney; it would mean taking them from other important jobs. I'm asking only for him to point the place out to us, then you can take him straight home. He'll be back in his bed in half an hour or so,'

Harry continued to protest.

'I'm sorry,' said Inspector Yapp, 'I assure you I wouldn't insist if it was not absolutely necessary. The sooner one has assembled evidence of a crime, the better the chances of catching the perpetrator. A policeman cannot afford to waste precious hours.' He bent towards the boy. 'You don't mind helping us, do you? There's nothing to be afraid of, Philip. You shan't be made to look at what you saw, we only want you to show us where it is.'

Mutely, Philip shook his head.

'It's better for him to go now than later,' Inspector Yapp said. 'Once it's over, he'll be able to put the whole thing out of his mind; it'll no longer haunt him.' The detective meant that he would no longer be haunted by the *memory*: the child understood him to mean he would no longer be haunted by the *ghost* of the dead woman — that is, haunted by the 'appearance' of her in his mind.

'Please, Dad,' he said. 'Please! I want to go.'

Which was how it came about that they went.

★ ★ ★

Philip walked between his father and the inspector through the crunchy wood. There was no moon — the D-shaped sickle in the sky had set hours ago, just after sunset. Two policemen walked ahead, their torch-beams shining through the trees. It was not easy to find the place in the dark. But suddenly something in the configuration of three tree trunks struck him as familiar.

'That's it,' he said. 'That's it.'

'You're sure?'

'Quite sure.'

'Then the constable can drive you and your father home; we shan't need you anymore,' said Detective Inspector Yapp. 'Thank you for your assistance, Philip; you did very well,' he said as he closed the car door upon them and watched them drive off. Then he went back to the beech trees.

The constables were standing at the edge of the cup-shaped depression. They looked up as their superior approached, and one of them called: 'There's nothing here, sir.'

'What d'you mean, nothing there?'

Yapp said sharply, quickening his steps.

'The kid must have dreamt it,' said the constable.

The inspector's eyes were not sad now; they were large with anger.

'The boy was not dreaming, Wilkinson. I spoke to him. He was quite genuinely disturbed.' He jumped down into the shallow pit, poking among the leaves with a stick. He bent, groped around, and picked something up. 'And this, very likely, is his ball. He didn't dream that he was up here playing with this, at any rate.' He climbed out. 'What did happen then?' he said slowly, half to himself.

Constable Barber said hesitantly: 'The one thing that did strike me as a bit odd was that he didn't run straight to his parents with his story but kept it to himself all that while. That doesn't sound natural to me, sir.'

'He didn't want his father to know he'd not been to the swimming baths with the rest of the school. You think that's unreasonable?'

'Seems a bit off to me, sir. His

behaviour seems to me like someone under the influence of drugs.'

'You think he may have been on a trip, imagined he saw a corpse, and not known it was only his disordered perceptions, is that it?'

'I thought it might be possible, sir. It seems to be happening all the time now, everywhere; schoolchildren taking drugs, I mean. He mightn't even realise it was a drug if some kid had pushed what looked like a sweet at him . . . What boy would refuse?'

'It's a feasible supposition, Barber,' said the inspector as the police car returned. 'And that would seem to be about as far as we can take it,' he added as they walked towards the car. 'We have no reason to pursue the matter any further. There's nothing to go on.'

★   ★   ★

Traffic Officer Gamley was feeling very cold. He had the impression that someone was thumping a road surfacer just behind his head. Cautiously he raised a hand to the back of his head, and something caught at his sleeve and scratched his bare hand. He appeared to be lying among brambles and nettles, and, since he could see the sky, deduced that it must be by the roadside. It occurred to him that he had had an accident. Methodically he tried moving first one leg then the other: they moved. He thought thankfully that at least his spine wasn't injured. Gamley lifted his head up a few inches and groaned aloud. The stars swam about like fish when he moved his eyes.

Sitting up was the worst bit, but he turned over and got on to all fours, and then to his feet. His motorcycle was on its side a few feet away. The front tyre was flat, and the two-way radio smashed. Otherwise, the torch-beam showed him, there didn't seem to be a scratch on it. He sat down on the saddle and leaned his aching head on his arms crossed upon the handlebars. It had not been an accident; he had been attacked.

Into the dull confusion in his mind, a

few random images made their appearance. Gamley began to remember — in pieces.

A general call had been put out to all traffic control concerning a break-in at Radwell House: all vehicles were to be stopped for questioning and searched. Gamley remembered that. The time had been one-thirty a.m. He looked at his watch: it was a few minutes past two. So he couldn't have been out for very long.

Radwell House was a handsome eighteenth-century pile a few miles from Southampton. It was not known yet how much had been taken, apart from a large fifteenth-century Flemish tapestry and several valuable paintings. Three cars had been seen to leave the grounds about twenty past one. It was believed that each had taken a different route, to lessen the risk of them all being caught.

At this point, Gamley recalled chasing to a halt a Cortina (and here he felt for his notebook and discovered it was not in his pocket). He spent some minutes searching for it along the roadside with his torch and, rather to his surprise, found it at last crushed into the mud and gravel by a wheel. He must have dropped it when they struck him down. It was very dirty and torn, but it verified to him that he had stopped them at one forty-five, and it gave the car number as BUF 888 E. It was on the way to Bournemouth, according to the driver, who had no driving licence and did not know the number of the car.

Gamley had a clear little picture of the driver's face by the yellow light of his torch: bold-featured, middle-aged, personable; but he fancied it was the other one who had hit him.

Yes, Gamley remembered flashing his torch into the back of the car and catching a glimpse of what appeared to be a spade, and had then said he would like to take a look in the boot. The key had been handed across to him by the other man, who had then climbed out of the car himself. Gamley had bent down to fit in the key, and at that moment his safety helmet had been knocked over his eyes and the universe had split open with a terrific *klonk* . . .

Gamley thought, *I must get back to the station*, and wondered how. There'd be hell to pay! He should never have attempted to tackle them on his own, but should at once have radioed back the car number as soon as he learned the driver did not know it and had no licence. He was lucky really that they hadn't killed him, but only cut his tyre and smashed his radio. He was surprised they'd bothered even to drag him off the road!

A faint glow appeared behind the elms at the end of the road. It meant a car was coming up the hill. He stood in its path with his hand held up.

'Hullo, Dr. Ford,' Gamley said. 'Could you drop me off at the station, if it's not too much out of your way? There's been an accident.'

'Anyone hurt?'

'Only me,' said Gamley, and laughed. 'I was just telling myself I was lucky not to have been killed.'

★   ★   ★

Douglas McMurdo was surprised to find himself on a Regency sofa. It took him a moment or two to realise that he was in Alys's living-room. He was cramped from the way he had been lying. He sat up stiffly, and wondered why the hell he had slept on the sofa instead of going to bed.

He walked with uneven steps to the bedroom, but Alys had not returned. The electric clock in the perspex cube by the bedside said five past six. He thought, *What a bloody godawful hour to waken on a Sunday morning. And where was Alys? What could have happened to her?* The very phrase was enough to send a ripple of unease across his mind. Could there have been an accident? Ought he to start phoning the hospitals, the police?

McMurdo stretched and went yawning over to the window. The distant sea and sky ran together in a milky haze, as though someone had forgotten to mark in the horizon. Below, the street was empty, except for a stationary milkfloat partially visible to him through the willows edging the sidewalk. The world had gone quiet. He felt suddenly unutterably depressed.

He badly needed some coffee and a hot bath.

A ginger cat streaked across the road as though it was being chased by some particularly ferocious dog, flew through the air like a winged Nureyev and landed on top of the wall, where it sat all at once as still as a statue. The absurdity of it charmed McMurdo, who felt all at once more cheerful. He noticed that it was a fine day. He slid open the window and uttered a thin miaow. The cat jumped down in a great hurry and disappeared from sight. He leaned out, but the cat had gone. He could see his blue Lotus below. There was a white Triumph to the right of it, a fawn Jaguar to the left, and beyond that a scarlet Mini. He glanced towards the lock-ups automatically and saw that Alys's garage was now shut. So *she was back*.

For the briefest moment his heart took a leap of pleasure, to be followed by a sickening lunge. She had come back but she had *not come in*. She had come back, and she had gone out again to spend the night with someone else. Or perhaps she had not even gone out again, but had spent the night here, in someone else's flat.

She must have seen his Lotus, she must have. His wrists were trembling as he leaned on the window frame. He drew back and closed the window with a bang. It was all over, then.

He scribbled below his message on the carrier-bag: *Sorry I couldn't wait.* And then crumpled it up and threw it into the waste bin.

Slamming the door, he ran down the stairs, without waiting for the lift, as though he was being pursued by some invisible demon.

5

It had been after three when Cynthia got home. At four she had taken a sleeping pill and had not heard Edmund return — if return he had. She was awakened at half past eight by the telephone, a call from No. 10 put through by one of the secretaries. Cynthia said, 'I don't know if he's awake, Dick; I haven't seen him yet. I've only just surfaced myself. But I'll give him the message.'

On her way downstairs to make her breakfast, she did just glance into her husband's room to see if he were there. He was heavily asleep, in a strange exhausted posture with one arm flung out. He looked, she thought, like a soldier lying on a battlefield.

It surprised her to see his clothes crumpled on the floor. He must have been damned tired or drunk last night: Edmund always put his clothes away when he took them off. She stooped and picked them up. The suit would have to be cleaned; there was mud on the front of the jacket, mud on the trouser ends. She couldn't imagine what he had been doing to get in such a state. She began to empty the pockets, laying his wallet, loose change, handkerchiefs, and all the other odds and ends on the chest of drawers. She moved softly from the room, carrying his shoes downstairs to clean.

She was drinking her second cup of tea when she heard the water running in his bathroom. When it stopped, she called to him. At the third call he appeared in the doorway, toweling his hair dry from the shower, and said: 'Hullo! Did you call?'

Cynthia was leaning against a pile of pillows, looking as fresh and fragile as a wild flower. He wondered how she managed it. Her breakfast tray lay across her knees and around her were spread the Sunday papers. It made Edmund's heart ache to see her. He wished ardently, perhaps more fervently than ever before, that it was possible to talk to her.

'The P.M. wants to see you at ten-thirty instead of eleven. Is that all right? I said it was. I didn't want to wake you; it was so late when you got back.'

'Did I wake you? I'm sorry, I did try to be quiet . . . Is there any tea left, do you think?' he asked, seating himself on the edge of her bed.

'I expect so.' She tipped the dregs out, filled the cup again with graceful movements, and passed it across to him. 'You haven't forgotten that it's Mrs. Roffey's weekend off, have you? So if you want me to pack for you, you'd better leave the things out and I'll see to it.'

'Thanks,' Edmund said, buttering a piece of toast. 'Where would you like to lunch today? If Mrs. R's not here, it would be less bother to eat out, wouldn't it?'

'Were you expecting me to have lunch with you? I'm sorry, I can't.'

He looked absurdly hurt. 'I thought you were coming with me to the airport.'

'Oh, we shall be back in plenty of time for that. I've arranged to be back by three. Half past at the latest.'

'The plane leaves at twenty past. I told you.'

'No, you didn't. I thought you were taking the ten to five.'

'That was the official time I'm supposed to leave. I'm taking the earlier plane to avoid — well, to avoid trouble.'

'You mean skyjackers and that sort of thing?'

'Oh, I don't suppose anything like that is going to happen; I just don't want innocent people to get hurt. Are you going to eat that other piece of toast?'

'No,' she said, pushing the tray across to him. 'Look, Ned, I'm sorry but it's not my fault you're taking an earlier plane, is it? I can't alter my plans now.'

'It doesn't matter. I can make other arrangements. If I seem disappointed, it's because I was hoping that for once in a way we might be able to have a talk.'

'We're talking now.'

'Yes. So we are,' he agreed. He took up the paper nearest to him and glanced at the headlines. He said casually, 'Do you know anyone with a black Mercedes?'

'No, I don't think so. Why?'

'I had the impression it was following me.'

'Well, you're surely more likely than I am to know who that might be. Perhaps it depends on what you were doing and who you were with at the time. It sounds as though I missed an opportunity,' Cynthia said with a laugh.

'Did you miss it? That's what I want to know.'

'Oh really, Ned! Are you suggesting I had you followed? I'd never do such a thing. Surely you know that.'

'That wasn't what you said the other day.'

'You can't count what was said in a row, Ned; don't be so silly. I wanted to get you to *agree* to give me grounds for divorce. You were so damned obstinate I lost my temper, that's all.'

'Is it obstinate not to want one's marriage broken up?' he said with a crooked smile. 'I don't happen to want to be divorced from you, that's all.'

'Why?'

'Because I fancy I'd be lonely without you.' He rose and picked up his towel. 'I must go and dress or I'll be late for Geoffrey.'

'If I don't see you again before you go,' she said, holding up her fragrant little face, 'have a good trip, and . . . best of luck.'

'Thank you.' He dropped a brief kiss on her cheekbone.

'Don't forget to put out your things,' she called after him. 'The shoes you wore last night are in the kitchen, if you want them. I cleaned them for you. The mud on them was as thick as the crust on a game pie. I can't think what you'd been doing,' she added from behind the paper.

'I had car trouble, I'm afraid. That's what made me so late.' He closed the door.

Cynthia lowered the paper and stared coldly across the room at her image in the dusky Venetian mirror. *He takes me for a fool*, she thought, *but I won't say anything. It isn't the moment to pester him when he has so much on his mind.*

She took up the paper once more, reading through half a column without taking in a single word of it.

★   ★   ★

97

Edmund Burke paused for a moment on the steps of No. 10 with a brief smile as the flashbulbs went off. The pressmen shot questions at him like a hail of arrows. Edmund held up a defensive hand.

'There's absolutely nothing to tell you. Ask me again when I come back,' he said good-humouredly, and turned away.

'See you at the airport, sir!'

'Can we have a statement, then?'

Edmund smiled and waved a hand in a gesture which might have meant acknowledgement or negation. He turned left out of Downing Street and along Whitehall, immersed in thought. The last-minute discussion with Geoffrey had been rather upsetting. The prime minister wanted Edmund to change his line of approach. He felt the situation in the Middle East needed to be dealt with more swiftly than Edmund's plan would allow for, before it could deteriorate still further.

It was Geoffrey Scowen's idea that Edmund should save time by *beginning* with a round table discussion with the U.A.R. heads of state, instead of (as Edmund was proposing) interviewing each ruler separately and getting from him some possible terms of agreement, before any general meeting was broached.

Geoffrey was right, of course, that all possible speed was necessary before the physical situation should change and render any progress towards peace they might have reached irrelevant and out of date. But Geoffrey did not understand oriental psychology, and Edmund did. You would never get the United Arab Republics to unite over acceptable peace terms — not in an open-ended discussion. The only way was through the back door, breaking down each one's resistance separately. Somewhat on the principle of the private bids put in at a Scotch auction, so that no one member would know what another member had committed his country to. The procedure might be lengthy, but, it seemed to Edmund, at least, that the prospects were more hopeful.

Edmund paused in his meditations to let a stream of people pour down the steps of a building and disperse. Something about them, a kind of old-fashioned

neatness perhaps, penetrated his consciousness as he stood there. It was
Sunday, he realised, and they were
coming out of church. A priest in a biretta
was standing in the arched doorway,
smiling and shaking hands with someone.
The sight of him reminded Edmund of
something he wanted not to think about:
Alys lying dead in an unmarked grave,
unhouselled and unshriven. He imagined
that for a practising Catholic there could
be no worse end.

The priest had vanished inside and all
the people had gone their ways. Edmund
began to mount the steps. He pushed
open the iron-studded door. The building
appeared to be empty except for the
painted plaster saints with their sweet
insipid faces and blank blue eyes, meekly
smiling down at the candles glittering in
their honour.

He became aware of a faint muttering
chant going on somewhere. He walked
quietly around and presently found it was
coming from a side chapel where a priest
was saying mass with his server. The only
worshippers were a middle-aged woman

in one pew and an old one in another: together they knelt, and rose, and sat down, and knelt again, mumbling their responses to God rather than the priest who was performing the ritual before their unseeing eyes, each alone in her private world. The server moved from one side to the other and back and forth in a kind of ritual dance. The priest raised two fingers in the classically hieratical gesture of blessing and made the sign of the cross, and whirled about, and bobbed once again to the altar, and went out, round a pillar and out of sight, with a whisk of his skirts.

Edmund waited for the women to finish their prayers and depart too, watching them gather together their things, turn in the aisle to genuflect towards the altar, and then patter towards the massive doors. He took the opposite direction: the way the priest had gone.

He found the priest in the sacristy, disrobing with the aid of his server. The server, being shorter than the priest, was having some difficulty in getting the cotta over his head, the priest addressing him meanwhile in an admonitory undertone. To which the server — a weedy unattractive youth with greasy hair and wire-rimmed spectacles — unctuously muttered back, 'Very good, Father,' and 'Just as you say, Father.'

It was he, though, who caught sight of the stranger standing in the doorway and drew the priest's attention to him — the priest having his back to the door. The priest swung round.

'Can I help you?' he said.

'I wonder if I might have a word with you?'

'Certainly. Come in, come in! But if it's for confession — '

Edmund said quickly: 'No, no. I'm not a Catholic. I just want to speak to you . . . on a private matter.'

'Would you like to come up to the presbytery?'

'It isn't necessary, Father — ?'

'Father Noone.'

'It'll only take a few minutes.'

'Very well. Run along then, Dennis. Where are you going, child?'

'To put the vestments away, Father.'

'Leave it, leave it. I'll put them away myself later.'

'Very good, Father, just as you say.' He scuttled out like a cockroach, and stood the other side of the door, still holding the handle so that the latch could not slide home. His oil-black eyes glistened behind their glasses.

Dennis Knockhouse had recognised the man the minute he saw him; recognised his voice the moment he spoke. Couldn't put a name to him, except that he was in the government in some capacity and was someone quite important. He'd seen him only the night before on the telly, only he hadn't been paying attention, as he'd been heating a tin of baked beans on the gas-rig for his tea. But what Dennis Knockhouse wanted to know, with an avid but quite meaningless curiosity, was what this man could want to see old Noone about. It excited him to know other people's secrets, however trivial they might turn out to be. It gave him a sense of power.

He was pretty sure Moony Noone hadn't a ghost of an idea who he was. He eased the door a fraction ajar and leaned his cheek against it.

'I was wondering if I, as a non-Catholic, can have prayers said for the repose of someone's soul?' the man was asking. It was for a Catholic, he went on, who had died suddenly without receiving the last rites.

What he really would like, if such a thing was possible, the man said, would be to have masses said 'in perpetuity' for the repose of her soul.

Her! thought Knockhouse. That made it interesting, though it would probably turn out to be some old aunt.

'You want a mass said on the anniversary of this person's death. Is that what you mean?' said old Noone. Dennis ceased to listen as he maundered on about it. Knockhouse heard him opening a drawer, and then Noone asking for the date of the person's death.

The man said: 'Yesterday. The 21st.'

'And the name of the departed?'

'Is that necessary?'

Old Noone said in his driest tone, 'Well I'm sure I don't know how one can pray for a person if one doesn't know who it is.'

'Forgive my ignorance, Father. The name of the dead woman is Mrs. Daneforth, Mrs. Hugh Daneforth — d a n e f o r t h,' he spelt out as the priest's pen scratched on the page.

'There!' said the priest. 'And your name?'

'Edward Smith.'

'You have done the right thing, Mr. Smith; God hears our prayers and He will be merciful; and now if there's nothing else I can do for you, I will ask — '

'Thank you, yes, just one thing,' the man called Smith said as quickly: 'If you would tell me what is customary in these circumstances . . . Is there a set charge perhaps?'

'We are not quite as venal as that, my son,' Father Noone said amiably. 'We don't charge for our prayers. A small contribution, perhaps, for those who can afford it, towards the cost of the mass; and there's always room in the poor-box for a few more coins; or maybe something towards the upkeep of the church building . . . '

Knockhouse heard the rustle of paper and smiled to himself. There was no one like old Noone for getting it out of them. And quite right too. The heathen fellow coming in here and asking his favours! He wondered how much Mr. Smith had given. It would probably stick to the lining of Noone's pocket anyway, thought Dennis, knowing chap that he was. He slid away hurriedly, hearing steps coming towards the door, and took cover behind a pillar.

The man who called himself Edward Smith came out first — only, Edward Smith was not, Dennis was almost sure, his real name. Edward sounded right but the surname was something with a B. More likely Bailey . . . or Baker. Yes, that was it, Edward Baker! Or no, he decided, that wasn't quite it either. But he'd probably remember it later and anyway it wasn't of any importance.

What was much more interesting was the sight of the notes in Father Noone's hand: there must have been thirty quid in fivers! Gawd! thought Dennis Knock-house enviously, imagine having that kind of money to fritter on masses for the dead. What a bloody rich bloke he must be!

He'd never have *anything*. It'd be tinned beans and instant coffee and powdered soup and tinned steak-and-kidney pie and fish fingers and frozen peas and other people's furniture and a shilling in the gas for ever and ever. He suddenly saw with a horrifying clarity that he would never find the wonderful first edition that was going to make him rich, the thought of which had kept him going for years, with the daily hope of stumbling upon it in someone's attic or at some out of the way sale. He'd been kidding himself, living in a dream world.

No one was ever going to read that piece in the paper about this twenty-seven-year-old secondhand-book dealer who had sold to the Bodleian for £54,000 a 2nd-century Greek papyrus fragment of St. John's Gospel. Or it might be a small handwritten volume in 17th-century script. Or an illuminated bestiary. Or

... or ... whatever it was it would be something rare and remarkable, and the finding of it was a notable instance of intuition and scholarship. Whatever it was, it transferred him in one leap into a different life as a highly respected antique dealer with his own shop in St. Martin's Lane — instead of the miserably cramped four-foot stall in the Portobello Road, which was all he could afford.

Poor bloody fool, Dennis thought with grinding self-contempt.

The church door banged, wakening Knockhouse from his sour disheartening glimpse of reality.

'Still here, Dennis?' said Father Noone.

'Still here,' said Dennis dully, and the words tolled like a bell in his head: *Still here, still here ... still ... here ...* as though there was nowhere else in all the world for him to be.

★ ★ ★

Originally it had been Cynthia's intention to drive Edmund to the airport, see him off, and then drive the Bentley back. It

108

was what she always did if she was not accompanying him abroad. What changed her mind was a quite unforeseen phone call the previous evening, after Edmund had left for the television studios and before Mark Nevinson arrived to take her to Grosvenor Square. It was a trunk call put through at the cheap rate after 6 p.m.

'Is that 01-748-9843?' a rough male voice had asked. And when Cynthia had said yes, it went on to say surprisingly: 'Well, I don't know who you are but I think I've got your dog. I come across him on me way home. He seemed to be wandering around loose. Only, he's got this number on his collar and I thought you'd like to know.'

'How very kind of you!' said Cynthia. 'I've been worried to death. I can't tell you how relieved I am to know he's all right.'

'I could see he was a valuable dog.'

'Yes, indeed.'

'I thought there'd probably be a reward but I didn't think it fair to hang on to him till he was advertised for,' the gentleman said in piously considerate tones. 'I'm an animal lover myself.'

'Oh good! Then would it be too much to ask you to keep him tonight? I could come down and get him tomorrow, if that's convenient to you?'

'Oh, I don't mind looking after him, don't worry about that. But I'll be out tomorrow morning. I fetch me old dad over to Sunday dinner. Wouldn't be back before about one. That suit you? Could make it a bit earlier, if you like.'

'I don't know yet where you live.'

'Blimey, nor you do. Voicey's the name, and I live at 22 Lower Meadow. It's a council estate in Torrington, near Pulborough, Sussex. Do you know that part?'

'Did you say Sussex?' Cynthia said incredulously.

'That's right,' said the man. 'Got it?'

'Yes, I've got it. Thanks awfully. And Mr. Voicey,' she called above the sound of the pips, 'you will give him something to eat, won't you?'

'Don't you worry, miss, I won't let him starve. He's already had the steak pie I'd got for my tea.'

Cynthia was blazingly angry with

Edmund. Why had he lied to her so stupidly? It was clearly impossible for the dog to have been lost in Hyde Park and found more than sixty miles away in Sussex two or three hours later.

This was why she said nothing to him about Beau having been found, the Sunday morning as he sat on her bed, merely telling him that she would not be able to take him to Heathrow. It wasn't that she had forgotten that Edmund was leaving that day. She genuinely believed he was flying by the later plane and she looked forward with malicious pleasure to seeing Edmund's face when he saw Beau in the car beside her. She imagined it would give him quite a shock, and serve him right.

However, as it happened, it hadn't worked out like that. It was not her fault that Edmund had chosen to go by the earlier plane. There was nothing she could do about it because there was no way she could get in touch with Mr. Voicey to let him know. Besides, there was Beau to be considered, the poor darling. No, as she had said to Edmund at the time, she really couldn't alter her arrangements now.

Which, as it turned out, was a pity.

Interlude

In a room high up in an ugly yellow Victorian house in Mornington Crescent, two men confronted one another.

'You failed!' The man, who spoke in a language that was not English, spat out the words in a tone of contempt, his black eyes flashing with suppressed rage.

'I deny that, comrade,' said the other in a forcedly calm and relaxed manner. 'The step I took, while I admit it was unplanned, I think you will agree was the only — '

'You failed to achieve the objective set you. That is what matters.'

'It was unavoidable. I did the best I could. No one could have done anything else in the circumstances. My only mistake was in thinking that the honourable English gentleman would behave as an English gentleman should and — '

'I am not interested in excuses or explanations. You failed our people. You failed the cause. It is up to you now to rectify your blunder. You will be given fresh instructions — and this time, comrade, you will carry them out to the letter. Listen to me carefully.'

With a noisy sigh, the other man subsided into a chair with a sulky expression on his face and prepared to listen.

6

By the time Cynthia had found Mr. Voicey's house, duly shown her appreciation, calmed the ecstatic dog, stopped at a pub for a toasted sandwich and a gin, and taken Beau for a run on the Downs, it had gone half-past three when she got back to London.

Her little red car was just turning into the mews which lay behind their house when a policeman held up his hand and stopped her. He came forward.

'Are you intending to enter the mews, madam?'

'Yes, I am.'

'May I inquire what for?'

'I don't see that it's any of your business, but my garage is in there.'

'May I know your name, please?'

'Mrs. Edmund Burke. What's going on?'

'I'm sorry, Mrs. Burke, but would you mind parking your car temporarily in front of your house? There's been a fire in the mews and it's still being dealt with. Very sorry to inconvenience you, but someone will be coming round to see you presently and they'll explain the situation.'

'Where was the fire?' she called after him as he walked away, but evidently he didn't hear. From where the car had stopped, she was just able to see into the mews; only, as she reversed into it, she could see in her driving-mirror a kind of blackened cavity where their garage was and a mess of black water running down from it. Funny of the policeman not to have told her, but perhaps he wasn't aware that it was their garage. He had said that someone would come around presently to explain. She drove round to Arundel Place. There was no space vacant in front of her house and she had to leave the car in a nearby side street.

Laden with odds and ends of shopping bags, and with Beau's leash wrapped round her hand, she was walking back to the house when a young man came up to her and said: 'It is Mrs. Burke, isn't it?'

Cynthia smiled at him vaguely, as was her way. She was not good at recognising people and preferred to simulate recognition than to cut them. She realised almost at once this time that she had made a mistake, for the young man followed it up by asking with an ingratiating smile if she could tell him what had happened.

She said: 'I'm afraid I don't know what you're talking about,' and quickened her step.

'We've been trying to get in touch with you ever since it happened,' the young man said reproachfully. 'Does Mr. Burke know about it?'

'I've no idea.'

'Can you tell me where I can get in touch with him?'

'No!'

'Oh, come on, Mrs. Burke. Give us a break! Do you think the fire at your garage was arson?'

'I don't know anything about it; I've only just come back from the country,' she said irritably. She ran up the steps and fumbled her key into the door.

'Mrs. Burke, please!' said one of the

men loudly from the pavement: and click-click went a camera as she turned her head. Cynthia went in and slammed the door.

She stood in the hall a moment, setting down her parcels, and thinking to herself the papers must be desperately hard up for news. She was unfastening Beau's lead when the telephone rang.

'Mrs. Burke?' a male voice said in her ear, and went on in a sympathetic but brisk manner: 'I am deeply sorry to intrude on your privacy at such a time, but is it true that Mr. Edmund Burke is dead?'

'What?' Cynthia stammered. 'Certainly not. What do you mean? Who are you?'

'Mr. Burke is reported to have been killed in a bomb explosion. If you haven't already heard, I must apologise most sincerely — '

Cynthia was listening less to his actual cliches of apology than the accent in which they were said, which at times seemed faintly foreign and at other moments vaguely mid-Atlantic.

' — so clumsy of me,' he was saying;

'but I was hoping you would be able just to confirm or deny it.'

'Who is speaking? Are you a reporter? What paper are you working for?'

He said plaintively: 'I'm only doing my job, Mrs. Burke. It's as disagreeable for me as it is for you. All I ask from you is a simple yes or no: is your husband dead or is he not?'

'How dare you speak to me like this! Go away. Leave me alone,' she cried in a high-pitched voice. Cynthia put down the receiver. She was trembling from head to foot. She opened the cupboard in the bureau-bookcase and with a shaking hand poured herself a stiff brandy.

Of course he wasn't a reporter. The man must have been one of those wretched perverts she had heard of who got their satisfaction out of distressing women either by obscene suggestions or by pretending that there'd been an accident and a child or husband had been killed. It occurred to her that she ought to inform the police. But at that moment the telephone rang again.

Cynthia stared at it without budging. It

119

rang on and on before finally ceasing.

She sat there trying to recollect the name of the couple she knew slightly who lived in one of the four mews cottages. Her name was Mirabel, and she did some sort of fashion designing and he . . . made jewellery, was that it? Hanley, that was the name.

Hastily she found the number and dialled before it could ring again. 'Mrs. Hanley?' she said. 'This is Cynthia Burke. I wondered whether you could tell me anything about the fire.'

'Yes, ma'am,' said Mirabel, who came from the deep south. 'I'm here to tell you that I was the one who gave the alarm and called up your fire brigade.'

'Really? How splendid. What happened?'

'Why, honey, I'd been working away all morning in my room and I'd jus' come down to get myself a bite to eat — '

'What time was that?'

'Why, I guess it would have been around two o'clock, say a quarter of. I was just fixing myself some coffee when there was this terrific *bang*. I thought maybe a gas main had burst or something. I simply dove for the door to take a look around, and there, my dear, was your garage just a mass of flames. Absolutely terrifying. You may believe me, honey, I did not hang around with my mouth open: I beat it to the phone. I have to tell you they made it in pretty good time, yes ma'am, but I guess there was nothing anyone could do.'

'Well, thank goodness you were there, or the whole mews might have burned down. Do you know what started it?'

Mirabel said vaguely that maybe someone had dropped a lighted match or a cigarette end into an open can of gasoline, which might have been what caused that big bang.

'You didn't see anyone running away from there?'

'No, I didn't. Could be I just missed them. Or maybe — ' Mirabel broke off abruptly. She had been about to say that maybe there had not been time for him to get away. But the thought was too horrifying to voice.

Cynthia said: 'How did the police get

into the act, anyway? They don't usually turn up at fires unless, I suppose, it involves a crime, like say arson.'

'Is that right!' Mirabel said courteously.

'You didn't happen to notice, did you, whether the Bentley had already left?'

'Well, no, honey, I can't say I did. Except . . . ' She hesitated. 'The police did take something out of there. But I don't know what it was; it was covered with a tarpaulin.'

'I see.' There seemed nothing else to say. Cynthia rang off. The 'terrific bang' and 'something' covered with a tarpaulin linked in her mind with the suggestions put to her by the earlier phone call of Edmund being killed in a bomb explosion. But it couldn't have happened like that, she told herself; it must only be a cruel coincidence. Edmund and his secretary, Martin, were on their way to Geneva. She had only to ring Martin's flat, for instance, to confirm it. So she did. Simply to rid herself of the niggling thought. And precisely as she had expected, there was no reply. She was still listening to the steady persistent burr-burr when there was a ring at the doorbell.

On the step was standing a well-built unsmiling man of fifty or so, who raised his hat and said he was Detective Chief Inspector Walker of New Scotland Yard.

'Scotland Yard!' Cynthia exclaimed. 'I thought you'd come to see me about the fire in our garage.' She smiled. 'Well, come in, anyway.'

From behind her, a large white dog leaped on him with a deep-throated bark. The chief inspector, who once many years ago had been a dog-handler, stood motionless.

'Sit, Beau!' said Mrs. Burke, hauling him off. 'Sit, you vile brute!' she cried, pressing him down. And to the detective she said with her beseeching smile: 'I'm dreadfully sorry. He really wouldn't harm a fly. But he is a bit hysterical today, having only just got home after being lost for twenty-four hours.'

'That's all right,' said Walker, holding out his knuckles for the dog to sniff. 'He's only a pup.'

'Do come in,' Cynthia said, leading him

into the small library as the right venue for that kind of interview. 'What was it you wanted to see me about?'

'We want to get in touch with Mr. Burke. I wonder if you could tell me where your husband should be at this moment?'

'About halfway to Geneva by now, I imagine.'

The chief inspector looked mildly surprised. 'Oh! What time did he leave?'

'He caught the 3.20 plane.'

'He did actually catch it, did he? You saw him off?'

It was Cynthia's turn to look astonished. 'Me? Well, no. But one supposes he must have caught it. I mean, otherwise, he would have rung from the airport, I expect.'

'Do you not usually see your husband off?'

'I daresay I would have done, but I happened to have a previous appointment. Actually, there'd been a bit of a muddle over his time of departure. I thought he was taking the 5.50, or whatever it was, and I'd made my arrangements accordingly. But it turned out that he'd never intended to go on that flight; he'd always meant to take an earlier one so as to avoid any possible trouble at the airport or on the plane from terrorists. He'd made it public that he was going on a later plane so it wouldn't occur to them he might go on an earlier one. A sensible precaution, only he forgot to tell me beforehand.'

'Had he received any threatening letters recently, do you know?'

'I shouldn't think so. These Arab terrorists are hardly the sort of people to kindly warn you beforehand that you're going to be kidnapped or assassinated. You know, of course, that he's gone to Geneva to negotiate peace talks with the Middle East heads of state. And I suppose the terrorists are in dread that he might succeed. So it would hardly be surprising if . . . ' Her voice died away. She stared at the detective while her thoughts ticked round. 'Has anything happened to my husband?'

'I hope not, Mrs. Burke.'

'Why are you here?'

'Your husband is a very important man. We have to take care of him.'

'He has his own private detective to do that.'

'I'm glad you reminded me, Mrs. Burke. Let's go back to the beginning. When did you see him last?'

'When he left the house this morning to visit the prime minister. That was about ten.'

'How was he going to the airport?'

'I don't know. He said he'd make his own arrangements.'

'By taxi?'

'I don't know,' she said, frowning. She added in a sudden brusque voice: 'It may interest you to know that I had a phone call just now asking me to confirm that my husband had been killed by a bomb. They wanted to know if it was true.'

The detective appeared to straighten his already perfectly upright back. 'When was this?'

'When I came in. Half an hour ago.'

'Do you know who it was?'

'Naturally not.'

'Would you please tell me exactly what

he said? It was a man, I take it?'

As accurately as she could remember, Cynthia recounted the conversation. 'Has he?' she said when she had finished. 'Has Edmund been killed by a bomb?'

'I don't know, Mrs. Burke.'

'I'd much rather be told. I shan't have hysterics or faint or anything, I promise you.'

'I shouldn't dream of keeping it from you. But we don't know. We've been trying to trace him. Which is why I was asking you if you knew where your husband might be.'

As though the light had suddenly dawned, Cynthia said: 'It's something to do with the fire at the garage, isn't it? The constable up there said someone would be coming to see me about it, and all this while I've been waiting for them to arrive. It never entered my head it could be somebody from Scotland Yard, and a chief inspector at that.'

Walker nodded. 'Fires don't usually start by themselves in a garage even when it's an accident. There has to be someone there to spill the petrol or drop the match; there has to be someone to turn the switch that's going to cause a short circuit.'

Cynthia got up and walked around, looking for the cigarette box. 'I thought the whole idea of a time bomb was that it didn't require anyone to activate it once it had been set.'

'Ah, yes, but that's been set in motion by the assassin.'

'All right,' she said, standing before him with the open box. (But he refused; he didn't smoke. Neither did Cynthia, but she took one now.) She blew out a stream of smoke. 'All right,' she repeated. 'What reason have you for regarding this fire as an attempt on my husband's life?'

Walker looked grave. He leaned forward. 'Somebody died in that fire, Mrs. Burke. It could have been an accident; we don't know yet. Forensic is looking into it now. For the presents we're regarding it as homicide.'

'You say somebody died. Who was it?'

'We don't know yet. He hasn't been identified. It would help if you could give me the name and address of your husband's dentist.'

'A Mr. Marcus of Wimpole Street.' Cynthia started to say, 'Why?' but thought better of it. With extreme precision she stubbed out her cigarette, as though it made her feel sick. She had to clear her throat before she could bring out the words she wanted to say. 'You mean there's so little left that's identifiable,' she said huskily.

'I'm afraid so, Mrs. Burke. The car was just — ' Walker opened his hands hopelessly and shook his head. He would not have described to her, even if he could, that twisted mass of metal.

'This person was in the car — the Bentley?'

'In the driver's seat, yes. It would appear that he had no time to save himself. Which suggests that turning the ignition, for example, detonated the explosive. He had no chance.'

Some emotion flickered over Cynthia's face, lids blinking away the image in the mind, lower lip momentarily shaking loose from its partner; she had immense control, the detective noted, keeping an eye on her hands (always more of a giveaway than the face) and saw the hand beneath the other hand screw itself into a fist, screwing itself up, tight, tight, holding it in . . .

Walker said: 'How could your anonymous phone-caller know it was a bomb when we don't even know it for certain yet ourselves? Just coincidence, do you think? Who had access to the garage besides yourself and your husband?'

'If you mean, who else had a key — no one.'

'Then how did the man get in to set the explosive?' He glanced at her curiously; she was staring at him.

'I let him in.' She passed her knuckles across her brow. There was a look of horror on her face. 'I think I must have. I'd forgotten all about it. It was when I was leaving this morning. This mechanic came up and said he'd been sent to fix the Bentley for my husband. It didn't occur to me to question it; Edmund had told me before he left that he'd had trouble with the car the night before — it had made him very late home. It seemed natural enough that he should have phoned a garage and asked them to send someone out to collect it.'

'Did he collect it, this mechanic?'

'I asked him if he was going to, and he said not if he could fix it there. I said, 'Did my husband tell you whether he wanted it back today? Because if so, you must have it here by half-past one at the latest.' And I told him where to leave the key when he'd finished.'

'Did you ask where he came from?'

'Oh, I may have done, but he could have said the name of any garage; I wouldn't have paid any attention.'

'You didn't recognise him as someone you'd seen around in the garage you habitually go to?'

'I can't say I did. But these young men drift in and out of that kind of job, don't they?'

'He was young, was he?'

'Youngish, I think. I didn't pay much attention. I was in a hurry to be gone. I had to get down to Sussex by one to collect poor Beau. But I'm afraid anyway I'm the sort of person who doesn't take

131

Leabharlanna Poibli Chathair Bhaile Átha Cliath
Dublin City Public Libraries

much notice of people. I'm just not good at knowing what people look like. I have difficulty in describing even people I know well.'

'All the same, you must have noticed whether he was dark or fair, tall or short, stocky or slender, long-haired or not?'

'Oh, he was dark, yes, I did notice that. Foreign.'

'Foreign!' exclaimed the chief inspector. 'A West Indian?'

'Oh no.' She frowned, trying to remember.

'If something should come back to you later, I should be glad if you'd let me know. Any little thing, like what he was wearing.'

'Overalls, I suppose.'

'Yes? What colour?'

'A sort of faded blue, I think.'

'Any name on them? Never mind,' he said in a comforting voice. 'Perhaps you'd be able to recognise him if you saw him again.'

'Yes, perhaps,' Cynthia said hopelessly.

'Anything distinctive about his voice?'

'No. He spoke quite well.'

'Anything like the voice of the man who spoke to you on the telephone?'

'Oh God!' she cried. 'I don't know, I don't know!'

'It's all right, Mrs. Burke. Not to worry. We'll find him,' he assured her with a conviction he was far from feeling within.

One thing, thought Walker as he rose to go. If she'd invented this mechanic, she'd have had him off pat, with red hair and a squint or whatever took her fancy.

'As soon as we have anything to report, Mrs. Burke, we'll let you know.'

She nodded, and just as he was leaving, said in a low wincing sort of aside: 'What do you yourself think, Chief Inspector — *is* the man in the car my husband?'

Walker looked at her compassionately. 'It is a difficult time for you, Mrs. Burke. You have my deepest sympathy. I think you should have some friend or relative to stay with you just now . . . Goodbye.'

The minute he'd gone, Cynthia went to the telephone. She would have rung Mark before if there'd been a moment. All the while the man from Scotland Yard was there, she'd been thinking of him. Never had she needed him more.

'Hello?' said his deep dear voice in her ear.

'Mark! Oh darling, it's Cynthia — '

'Why, hello!' he said, which was not the way he usually greeted her. It meant that he was not alone. But today Cynthia simply didn't care.

'Something terrible has happened, Mark. I must see you.'

'Why, sure,' he said. 'What's the trouble?'

'It's Edmund. Can you come round?'

'I have some people here right now; but I'll be over as soon as I can.'

'For God's sake, get rid of them, Mark. I'm desperate. I can't be alone, I shall go mad. Please, darling.'

'Well now, you just hold everything till I get there.'

Cynthia started to say 'I think he's dead, Mark,' but a click told her he'd hung up. Slowly she put down the receiver. Tears began to rain silently down her cheeks, streaming out of wide pale sea-green eyes. When she cried, it was without any of the usual ugly painful signs of emotion. She cried, Edmund always said, like a mermaid.

She felt dreadfully alone, and afraid. Afraid of the guilt and remorse which might be lurking somewhere in the depths of her mind, only waiting to spring out and make her wretched. Yet why should she feel guilty? Edmund had behaved no better to her. Worse really, if one counted the number of offences. The only difference was that he had never made it a reason to break up his marriage. It was true that Cynthia had wanted to be free of Edmund, but she had not wanted anything like this to happen to him. She had never wished him dead. Or not in such a horrible way.

'How vile you are! What a hypocrite,' she muttered, getting to her feet and restlessly pacing the room. 'You're really not in the least upset about poor Edmund, all you're thinking about is your mean little self and how his death — if he *is* dead — will affect you. You really are a first-class bitch, aren't you? Have you nothing else to show for thirteen years of marriage? Not one genuine sign of grief?

'I loved him once, didn't I? Wasn't it real? If it was real, why is there nothing left of it now? Have I never really loved anyone but myself? Never in all my life? Not even Mark? Do I only love what he thinks I am?

'No, no, no!' she cried, turning from this relentless picture. 'It isn't true! I'm not like that! I'm in shock, that's what it is.'

Cynthia pulled a handful of petals off the roses and inhaled their velvety scent. In shock. Numb. Closing in on herself like some sort of sea anemone in self-protection. Shrinking from the conflict, the conflict of the mind between the dread of grief and the shameful guilt of un-grief at the prospect of a new life opening for herself and Mark. Freedom, excitement, a richness to life she had never before experienced —

Again she shrank from her thoughts in horror. *Life!* She was thinking about her *own* life, her own pleasures and satisfactions and all the intoxications of personal life, while Edmund lay *dead* . . . burnt up, unrecognizable. And everything that he had stood for, worked for, given himself to, had come to an abrupt end, left unfinished, in ruins . . .

Cynthia screwed her eyes tightly shut, running from the room as though she could run away from her thoughts, escape from that insistent voice inside her that was saying: 'Cry, damn you! Suffer! Weep!' She didn't understand these mysterious imperatives, but they terrified her.

Blindly she opened the front door and stumbled down the steps — into the arms of Mark Nevinson on his way in.

'Oh Mark!'

Suddenly she was shaken with violent sobs, overwhelming her the way a child, who has faced with great courage some appalling situation, will succumb instantly to its childish terrors the moment its parents appear on the scene. But Lord Nevinson could not know that. Only Cynthia could know she was crying for herself, not over Edmund.

He took her inside. Took her in his arms. 'Why, Cynthia honey, what is it?'

'Oh, darling, I'm so glad you're here! It's been so dreadful . . . Reporters

'. . . and a dreadful man on the phone . . . and a chief inspector from Scotland Yard questioning me for hours . . . '

'What about, honey?'

'*Edmund*. Oh Mark, they think he's been killed.'

'Killed! How?'

'Well, assassinated. They can't be certain yet, but they think a bomb was planted in the Bentley. The whole place went up in flames.'

'But that's too ghastly! My poor darling, what an awful thing to happen. Poor Edmund. I can't believe it. What did you mean, they *think* he's been killed? Surely they know whether a person's dead or not?'

'The body of someone was found in the car wreckage; they can't be sure yet whose it is.'

'But this is frightful! They had no right to come and tell you your husband was dead when they're not sure. What steps have they taken to find out if Edmund is still alive?'

'I don't know. But who else would be in the car?'

138

Mark asked Cynthia for the number and t.o.d. of Edmund's plane and went to the phone.

Cynthia felt that kind of relief we feel when someone takes over. While he was on the phone, she fixed them both a drink. He came back quite soon, his dark face serious.

'Edmund wasn't on the plane,' he said. 'It looks bad, Cynthia. Listen, you can't stay here alone. You must get away for a day or two.'

'Get away? Why? Can't you stay with me, Mark?'

'I couldn't do that, honey. It wouldn't be right.'

'Who would know? Darling, you don't know how much I need you.'

He smiled at her sadly. It didn't shock him that she should say such things. He thought only how innocent she was, as naïve as a child.

'How about your sister's?'

'Elspeth?'

'She's fond of you. And it's well out of the way; the press aren't likely to track you down there. I'll ring her up while you pack a case, and then I'll drive you down. How's that?'

'Does that mean I won't see you? No, if I have to go I'll take my own car. I don't want to be a prisoner.'

'I shouldn't,' he said. 'If the car is here, the press won't realise you've gone away. I don't want you to be badgered. I'll ring you twice a day.'

★   ★   ★

The first thing Chief Inspector Walker did on his return to the Yard was to send two of his men to make inquiries at every garage within a half mile radius of Edmund Burke's house if a mechanic had been sent to bring in Mr. Burke's car for repair. Not that he had much hope of getting an answer. One could be pretty sure that if Mr. Burke had not contacted the garage which usually attended to his motor, he would not have gone to any other garage. And that meant that whoever the mechanic was, he would most likely be the man who had fixed the explosive.

140

The whole business of the mechan.
puzzled the detective. It seemed so improbable that he wondered if there had been
such a person. Mrs. Burke's vagueness
bothered him. She had been so extraordinarily calm. She could hardly have shown
less emotion if they had been discussing
the death of someone unknown to her. He
wondered if the reason for her indifferent
attitude was that she had realised as clearly
as he did himself that she might have been
the intended objective and not her husband. If her plans had not been changed,
it might have been Mrs. Burke sitting in
the driver's seat, Mrs. Burke the one to
have been killed.

One had then to ask, 'Who?' and,
'Why?' Particularly why. Why should
anyone want to get rid of Edmund
Burke's wife? The obvious answer where a
woman was concerned was a husband or
lover.

Walker knew something of Edmund's
reputation with women, and quite by
chance someone had mentioned recently
in his hearing the current gossip about
Mrs. Burke and Lord Nevinson. One

would imagine that civilised people in the free society of the day would be able to arrange these things quietly through the divorce courts, but Walker was no innocent; he knew that this was far from always being the case. The rich and the powerful tended to be like spoilt children, determined to have their own way at all costs, believing that their wealth and power would protect them.

It was an unequalled situation for a man with murder in his mind. The idea of the Arab terrorists making an attempt on the life of the secretary of state for Mediterranean affairs had been so well planted in the public's consciousness that it would be natural for everyone to jump to the conclusion that that was precisely what had taken place. If Mrs. Burke had been killed, it would only have seemed an unfortunate blunder. No one would dream that it might have been the original intention of the murderer.

A sergeant put his head round the door. 'Sir, if you're not too busy, the press are waiting for some kind of statement from you about the Warwick Street garage fire.'

'Oh lord!' said Walker, coming from behind his desk. 'I'll see them myself.'

'Sorry to have kept you waiting, boys,' the detective chief inspector said as he walked briskly down the corridor towards them. 'Trouble is, I've nothing to tell you yet. So far we've not been able to identify the dead man, and until we do, until we know whether the secretary of Mediterranean affairs has in fact been murdered, I have to ask you on the prime minister's instructions not to leak out anything about the incident. You shall have the whole story, I promise, as soon as it breaks.'

And with that they had to be satisfied. Those who had already got in something of the story had to go back to their papers and kill it.

*   *   *

The Lewises of Old Chantry, Torrington were having a few people in for drinks that Sunday evening. They had people in most weekends if the children were there. The children invariably brought friends down with them, and Mrs. Lewis liked to mix them around with the local breed.

Her eyes roamed placidly among them now, as they stood on the paved terrace with their drinks, the declining sun burnishing their faces or setting fire to the hair of those perched on the stone balustrade which divided the terrace from the lower garden.

No one was looking at the roses, which was a pity, Mrs. Lewis thought, but only natural. Young people preferred to look at one another. She noticed with disapproval that the bank manager and the local CID inspector — such charming men, both of them — were talking to each other, and probably boring themselves to death, poor things. That would never do.

Deftly Mrs. Lewis separated them, and took the bank manager away to admire the roses. Detective Inspector Yapp, left on his own, looked around and was rather taken with a dark girl with long glossy black hair. She looked both smart and exotic in a slim black dress printed with brilliant green leaves and elegant black sandals at the end of her slender legs. No bits of jewellery hanging from her ears or round her neck, not even a ring: he liked that.

'Have you tried these cheesy things?' he said, shaking a dish at her invitingly. 'They're rather good.'

Her eyes, he noticed when she smiled up at him, were as green as emeralds, and in an unaccustomed flight of poetic fancy he thought, *They're the only jewels she needs*.

'I don't seem to have seen you round here before. Are you from London?'

She nodded. She was a friend of Jenny's, the Lewises' daughter. They worked on the same women's magazine. And her name, she said, was Pauline — Pauline Bury. 'And you?' she asked.

'Oh, I'm just a local yokel, name of Alan Yapp.'

'What do you do?'

'I'm a policeman,' Yapp said reluctantly. It was only the young, people of about the age of this girl, who hated and despised the upholders of law and order, but Yapp didn't want to see that look on this girl's face. 'A detective inspector, actually; Regional Crime Squad.'

'Now that is fascinating. It must have been in my stars this week, our meeting like this, because I have a puzzle for you to solve. Why don't we get ourselves another drink and sit down somewhere. I went for a tremendous walk with Dick this morning and my legs feel like spaghetti.'

I believe she likes me, Yapp thought, going off to collect the drinks. When he found her again, she was sitting on the steps outside the French windows, staring contemplatively at her out-thrust feet. He sat down beside her. She seemed to be lost in thought. Gently, without speaking, he put the glass into her hand.

'Do you like these sandals?' she said inconsequentially, turning a slim foot for his consideration.

'Very much. I was just admiring them.'

'They are rather divine, aren't they? And they fit me perfectly. They might have been made for me. Which you have to admit is an incredible piece of luck, considering I found them by pure chance.'

'Chance?'

'I literally picked them up this morning. I practically fell over them. There they were, the little beauties, lying on the ground simply asking to be taken home.' She shot him a sharp look. 'You're not going to be disagreeable, are you?'

'I hope not.'

'It is finders keepers, isn't it? You're not going to tell me I ought to have handed them in.'

'I'm off duty,' he smiled at her. 'Obviously they were meant for you. They look charming on you.'

'But the mystery I want you to solve is, how did they come to be there?'

'No great mystery, really. You'd be surprised at the things one finds littering the countryside.'

'You're right; I would be surprised if anyone threw shoes like these away. They happen to be *brand new*. And not only brand new but *hand-made*. I've never had a pair of hand-made shoes before. People don't just chuck away things like this.

Why should they?'

'They were hurting their owner. She couldn't stand them another minute. So, 'The hell with them!' she said, and kicked them off.'

'All right. If you like. But why *leave* them there? No one would do that, would they? They must have cost anything from fifteen to twenty guineas, maybe more, I don't know. Besides, what did she go home in?'

'She had another pair in the car for driving in,' he suggested.

'Shoes for driving in would have been more suitable for walking in up there. I shouldn't care myself to go tiptoeing among the brambles and tree roots in these.'

'Where was this, then?'

'Up in that little wood by the common from where one can see Chanctonbury Ring.'

'Do you mean Torrington Common?'

'Is that what they call it?'

'And that was this morning? What sort of condition were they in when you found them? Did they look as if they'd been there some time?'

'Oh no. Practically not a mark on them.'

'May I see them?'

'By all means,' she said, slipping one off and handing it to him. 'Subject it to your austere professional scrutiny.'

'My austere professional scrutiny requires them both,' Yapp said, holding out a hand for the other. Scrawled in gold inside the sole was the name of one of the great shoemakers of the world, whose name was known even to the provincial Yapp. A code number was stamped inside the shell of the heel. He turned the sandals over curiously. As Pauline had said, they were practically unmarked. He noticed a few faint scratches drawn along the back of the heels. There was so little to the pretty fragile objects that there was not much he could learn from them. He gave them back to her.

'Interesting,' he said. 'It looks as if there may be more to it than meets the eye. Tell me, did you have the impression that they'd been accidentally dropped there, or had they been placed there deliberately? Were they together, or was one here and one there?'

She thought for a minute, a small frown wrinkling her brow.

'They were together,' she decided, 'about that much apart.' She held up her thumb and forefinger about three inches apart. 'Kind of on their sides, with the heels back to back and the toes pointing away from each other east and west, like Charlie Chaplin.' She smiled, hoping he would laugh at the picture she had conjured up, but the man was now looking quite serious. 'Have you a theory, Holmes?'

'What?' He came back from a somewhere a long way off and smiled at her. 'Watson, can you leave your practice for a few hours?'

'Easily. I have hardly any patients left. It's my old wound, you know.'

'There are some interesting features in this case, which with your assistance I should like to examine more closely, my dear Watson.'

'How can I help you?'

Yapp said in his ordinary voice: 'I want you to show me where you found these shoes. You won't have to walk this time, and it's not far by car. After that, perhaps we could have dinner together.'

'Are you serious? Do you really want to see where I found them?'

'Certainly I do. You've challenged me to solve your mystery and I've taken it on, so it's only fair to let me examine the evidence. There may be something more to find up there. It may even turn out to be something more important than a little psychological puzzle, you never know. I might even have to impound the sandals as evidence.'

'Evidence of what, for goodness sake?'

'Of a crime, my dear girl,' Yapp said, helping her to her feet with such a grave expression that, of course, she did not believe him and thought he was joking.

2nd Interlude

The air in the upper room of the ugly yellow-brick Victorian house was thick with tobacco smoke. There were four men in the room waiting on a fifth, who at this moment entered.

'Comrades,' he said, by way of greeting.

'You're late.'

'My dear Ziadeh, I didn't know there was going to be a meeting. You said simply that you wanted to see me. You should have warned me.'

'It is sufficient that you are here now. Sit down, Shehab. We are here to discuss the business you undertook to carry out — '

'Was ordered to carry out,' interjected Shehab.

'Ordered to carry out and undertook to do so,' emended the other. 'We want to hear what you have to say in your defence.'

'Do I need to defend myself? I did what

152

I was told to do. I carried out my instructions to the letter.'

'You failed.'

'You can hardly blame me for that.'

'You failed for the *second time*, comrade. We can't afford mistakes of that kind. You should realise that the position is too serious.'

The man with the drooping moustache who was standing by the window gazing through the dusty pane half-turned to say: 'It makes us look such fools.'

'That is hardly the point, comrade,' Ziadeh said sternly. 'The point is that our situation is critical, and this blunderer has bungled it again.'

'Blame the methods, comrade Ziadeh,' said Shehab. 'When are we going to face up to the fact that our methods never do succeed; they only make a big noise? Statistics-wise, we are extremely unsuccessful in attaining our ends. It works out at 20%, comrades — one in five. You are too old-fashioned in your approach. It is too late in the day to play at cowboys and Indians. This is a nuclear world, a world of ultimate destruction, and we must learn from it, comrades, that if we want to destroy, there are other means that are more thorough than going bang-bang.'

The moon-faced man sprawling in the only armchair said: 'Comrade Shehab has been over here so long he is getting Christian ideas.'

'What do acts of terrorism achieve?' Shehab demanded hotly. 'Temporary consternation and then increased resistance. No one is impressed, no one is converted to the rightness of our cause, in fact we lose sympathy. What do we gain? Occasionally the rather messy loss of one of our enemies. It isn't good enough, comrades, it isn't serious. Does no one recognise how desperate our situation is? Or is it that in our heart of hearts we do not believe we can possibly gain our ends, and so the only thing we are prepared to do is to make a big show of anger and determination, like a child screaming defiance at its nurse when it is time to go to bed — is that not how it is in reality?'

'Well,' said comrade Ziadeh with a sour smile, 'I thought we had come here to examine the extent of comrade Shehab's culpability in his failure to assassinate a certain person, not to have to listen to a lecture from him on what he considers to be the misguided directives of people more experienced than himself. I apologise to you, comrades.'

'I beg your pardon,' said Shehab stiffly. 'In my concern for the suffering of our people, I forgot myself.'

The man who had been sitting hunched and motionless in the dark corner, so quiet he had been forgotten, without raising his head, now spoke: 'I should like to hear what the comrade proposes before we condemn him out of hand.'

There was an awkward pause. Their faces turned towards Shehab, who said: 'It is a simple principle, like judo, comrade Mahmoud, where the enemy's own strength is turned against him. Only in my system, it is the events of the man's own life which are used to destroy him; they act like a lasso around him, and the more he struggles, the more helpless he becomes. He is done for without ever knowing how it happened.' His teeth gleamed with pleasure.

'Is it anything more than an idea? Has it ever been attempted? Does it work?'

'It is already underway now. Wait a little, comrade Mahmoud, and you will see for yourself how prettily it unfolds.'

And suddenly even comrade Ziadeh was laughing.

7

A cart track separated Andrew Meyrick's farm from the Cahoon property, some ten miles north of Petersfield. Today, Monday, seven acres of the Cahoon estate became his. Andrew gulped down a cup of scalding tea, stamped into his wellingtons, and taking one of his farmhands, went to inspect his new piece of land. According to the agreement, the first thing he had to do was to sink a heavy wire fence round it to separate it from the Cahoon estate. These seven acres were at the back of Cahoon's place, and their absence would not be noticeable — except in so far as it might make the property easier to sell.

The Cahoons, a stockbroker and his wife, had emigrated to the Bahamas some four years previously. They had lingered on in England for eighteen months trying to sell their elegant old stone-built house, and at last had decided not to wait any longer. They left the property in the hands of the agents at £28,000. The right person was bound to come along, they felt, just as they had themselves some fifteen years earlier and fallen in love with it. They had tried to keep the place unspoiled, rendering it comfortable without marring its character — no swimming pools for George and Justine. Justine had created a garden of rare distinction and subtlety. The whole place should have appealed to anyone of refined taste. But no such person came forward to buy it. The house hung on the market. The few firm offers which were made always fell through before contracts could be exchanged.

It became evident that nine acres to go with a house of three reception rooms and five or six bedrooms, with stables, garages, and a variety of outhouses, was too much for the average well-to-do family to carry. On the other hand, the property was too small for a country hotel or small school or anything of that sort.

And meanwhile, the property deteriorated. The garden had 'gone back';

unpruned, the fruit trees in the orchard had almost ceased to bear, and ivy gripped their limbs. The grass grew rank, thistles and docks took possession, trees grew into a thicket. The house itself was on its way to becoming a ruin, its window frames rotting as sun and rain peeled off their protective paintwork; the rain had got through a place in the roof where a couple of tiles had blown off in a storm three years since, leaving patches of leprous damp inside.

The Cahoons would have wept to see it, only they were too busy with their new house on Caicos to worry about the old one. Except when they wanted the money it would have brought. So when the agent suggested selling off some of the land to make the estate more compact and manageable, George agreed, with the proviso that the land should be taken from the north side and was not to be used for building land. Which suited Andrew Meyrick very well, and that was how he came to purchase it. He had indeed been after the land for years in a discreet backdoor way. Farmers always felt they could do with a little more land to, as it were, round things off, the way financiers could always do with a little more money.

Andrew and Norman stumped round in a fine drizzle, appraising and considering, measuring and calculating how many posts and how much wire would be needed. Some larking boys had evidently broken into the lower acres. There were tyre marks in the mud by the gate, and a couple of pegs that kept in position the wire marking the boundary had been pulled loose. Not that it mattered. They couldn't do any damage. And there'd be no more getting into it once Meyrick had fenced it in.

At eight they went back to the farm for the rotavator to break up the soil round the boundary to make it easier to sink the wire and the posts. 'Looks as though someone's already been doing a bit of digging,' Norman remarked as they made their way through the belts of hazel and willow in the bottom acre.

Meyrick grunted absently.

'Looks like a grave, dun' it?' said

Norman. 'Could be some cheeky bugger buried a dog there,' he muttered. 'Or mebbe a horse.'

'The Cahoons used to keep horses in the old days,' Meyrick said vaguely. 'You wouldn't remember.'

'Couldn't be one of theirs,' said Norman, and he let the gate fall to behind them. 'It's new.' Three yards ahead, Mr. Meyrick was saying to himself that the best thing he could do was to grub up the whole lot, turn it over, and put it down to kale or beet for next year. Though how he was ever to find the time . . .

His boy came into the yard to shout, 'Mum says brekfus is ready.'

'Tell her I'll be in presently,' said his father, disappearing into a shed.

It was when Andrew was walking across the lower field to see how Norman was making out with the trenching for the boundary fence that he noticed for himself the cuts that had been made in the earth some ten yards from the gate. It was a somewhat irregular oblong; like a kind of grave, as (it now came back to him) Norman had suggested. Someone

161

had lifted off the topsoil and then carefully replaced the matted turves of couch grass, rye, and weeds. Sharp of Norman to have seen it. Andrew wondered what they'd been up to, whoever had done it. It was too big for a dog and too small for a horse. Andrew raised a couple of turves with the toe of his boot and kicked them aside, then a few more.

At one end, four little highly coloured worms protruded from the loose earth — bottle green, yellow, scarlet, and dark blue. They were soft to the touch, the twisted woollen fronds fringing the end of a scarf or rug.

Meyrick bent and scooped the earth away with his hands. It wasn't buried very deep and it didn't take him long to uncover a tartan rug enfolding some bulky object. A silken strand of blonde hair clung to one edge. Meyrick's heart turned over. He didn't need, didn't want, to see any more. He went back to the farm and called the police.

He had to be there, of course, when they arrived, to show them what he had found. Inside the rug was the naked body of a young woman in a crouching posture, her ash-blonde hair hiding her face. The photographer took his careful studies of the scene before the police moved the body.

'Ever seen her before?' someone asked Meyrick casually.

'I don't know. Can't tell like that. Her hair all over her face.'

One of them stooped and gently pulled the tresses aside.

'Recognise her now?'

The wide dead eyes were rolled back, staring up at him. 'Must have been a good looker, poor thing. No, I never seen her.'

The inspector came up to him. 'We'll have to seal off this piece of ground for the time being, Mr. Meyrick, including the entrance. We'll try not to hold you up any longer than we need.'

Andrew said suddenly: 'There were some tyre marks up there, Mr. Roxborough. I half noticed them when we came in first thing. Noticed it, I suppose, because no one uses the path except us. It doesn't lead anywhere, y'see. Any vehicle coming up this lane would turn to the left, to my farm, not to this end. Unless it might be the odd courting couple.'

'Let's go and look.'

'Daresay they be pretty messed up by now,' Andrew said apologetically. He was right.

'Oh well, we can't win 'em all,' said the inspector. 'You wouldn't have noticed what kind of tyre marks, would you?'

'Can't say I did. Didn't take all that notice. Thought it was some of these here yobbos mucking around on their motorbikes. It was only my idea, mind, when I found the pegs yanked out that was keeping the boundary-wire in place.'

'Where?'

'Over yonder,' said Andrew, pointing. 'But I stuck 'em back now. Wouldn't do no good for you to go looking, me and Norman been tramping all over it with our big feet. Sorry.'

'You couldn't know.'

'More's the pity, though. Seems likely whoever buried that poor lass there fell over the wire in the dark. Yes, well, you'll want to make your own deductions. Well, if you don't need me any more . . . '

'Not for the present, Mr. Meyrick.'

'Hope you catch him, whoever he is,' Meyrick called over his shoulder as he tramped off.

★　★　★

Inspector Roxborough was in the mortuary with Dr. Grout, listening to the abrupt remarks he dictated to his assistant as he worked.

'Any idea yet how long she's been dead?' he asked presently.

'About forty-eight hours.'

'Which would make it sometime Saturday. Do you know yet how she was killed?'

'Strangled,' said Dr. Grout.

'Manually?'

'Look,' said Dr. Grout, standing aside and pointing with his scalpel, 'you'd hardly notice that crease round her neck, would you? It's cut into the flesh so deeply that the cuticle has closed round it.' He leaned across and, picking up a pair of forceps, dipped them into a shallow vessel. There was a light metallic tinkle as he lifted the object out. It gleamed silvery in the pale sunlight filtering through the glass roof as he held it up. 'This is what was used,' he said. 'It's the fashion now to wear such chains with some ornament hanging from them. Though they're not usually as finely wrought, or made of platinum.'

'You think she was wearing it?'

'No question about it. It was probably supporting a fairly heavy pendant by comparison; the pattern of the chain had left a faint impress on the skin just below the nape of the neck.'

'The chain is broken,' observed Roxborough.

'The pendant was wrenched off.'

'It could have been for the sake of the pendant she was killed, then. Could have been valuable if it was made up of precious stones.'

'The chain was twisted at the back of the neck so tightly that it was embedded in the flesh. That was why it wasn't visible to the casual glance. The two ends of the chain hung down at the back of her neck and were concealed by her hair.'

The inspector frowned, trying to imagine how this awkward action could have been performed. One would have to be behind the woman for it to have been pulled with such strength and knotted behind the neck. But the pendant would have been in front. The murderer had then to grab it from the front and swing it round his victim's neck.

'I don't see it,' he muttered. 'Any indications of assault otherwise?'

'No.'

'Did she put up any resistance? Any scrapings of blood or skin under the fingernails?'

'I have not had time yet to analyse the scrapings. But don't be too hopeful. Death would have been practically instantaneous, you know.'

'Too quick for her to put up a fight?'

'It looks like it.'

'Someone she knew then.'

'Could be,' agreed the pathologist, stripping off his rubber gloves and throwing them into the sink.

'Taking that in conjunction with the method used, it would seem to have been an unpremeditated crime, an act of impulse. Something she said that angered or alarmed him perhaps, and he grabbed at the chain in sudden rage or fear . . . Don't mind me, Dr. Grout, I'm just thinking aloud,' Roxborough said, rubbing his nose.

'Perhaps, Inspector. But it was very expertly done. It might quite easily have been bungled, but it appears to have been carried out neatly and swiftly, as it happens.'

'That might have been his good luck, I suppose. That curiously foetal position she was in, you don't think that could have been in self-defence? That she herself brought her knees and hands up like that?'

'If she was naked at the time, and if the murderer made a frontal attack on her, yes, it could be. Knees brought up to her chin and elbows bent. But then one would expect her face to be contorted.'

'And it isn't,' Roxborough agreed. 'So, why the posture?'

'I think I can explain that. It suggests to me that the crime, whether intentional or unpremeditated, occurred in some place where it would be liable to discovery. Your man had to get the body away. She was folded up like that, I would say, to fit into the boot of a smallish car. And then of course rigor mortis probably intervened before it was possible to remove her. By the time she came to be buried, the body would have become fixed in that position and could not be straightened out.'

'Yes, I see. Was it a sexual assault?'

'There are no signs which would indicate that.'

'You mean, she might have been stripped in order to make it appear to have been a sexual murder?'

'It is possible.'

'So it might have been someone known to her, someone of whom she was unafraid. She wasn't pregnant, I suppose, or anything like that?'

Grout shook his head.

'Any ideas about who she might be?' asked Roxborough hopefully.

'My assistant has,' said Dr. Grout with a snort of sardonic amusement. 'He says he thinks he's seen her on the infernal machine, an actress or something.'

'Well, that's a useful tip,' the inspector said politely. 'I don't view myself; don't have time for it. Anything else?'

'There's her description,' said the pathologist, reading it off: 'Height: five feet, five and a half inches. Eyes brown. Hair blonde. Skin olive. No scars or distinctive marks. Aged between twenty-four and twenty-six.''

'It doesn't tell one much.'

'There's still the rug. We may get quite a lot from that. There's some mud and dead leaves and a twig or two caught in it, and it's covered in white dog hairs. There were even some in the woman's hair. But I'll need another twenty-four hours before I can say if there's anything definite to be learned from the rug.'

'We haven't learnt much about her so far; we could hardly know less,' sighed Roxborough.

'I daresay that was the murderer's intention.'

Roxborough said suddenly: 'You think *that* might be why she was stripped naked? So as to divest her of anything that could be identified?'

'More than likely, I should say. I ought to mention that the skin on her right wrist is considerably lighter in hue in one place, where she habitually wore a watch. So unless the motive was robbery, as you suggested earlier, that would appear to be why it was removed.'

'But then why, after going to all that trouble, leave her wrapped in a rug? It doesn't make sense.'

'Not yet, it doesn't,' agreed Dr. Grout as he drew a sheet over the dead woman.

'It would seem to be a case of *Cherchez le chien*,' said Roxborough with a dry laugh.

★   ★   ★

It was hardly the moment Elspeth would have chosen to have her sister flung on their doorstep when she and Arnold were entertaining a houseful of guests. Apart from anything else, it would make the number uneven at table. But she had no choice in the matter. Lord Nevinson never asked if it was convenient; he simply announced that he thought Cynthia ought to get away from London for a day or two and he would be bringing her down himself.

'Ask him to stay to dinner, and then your numbers will be even,' said Arnold when she told him.

'As a matter of fact, I did. I knew you'd want me to. But he said he couldn't. He had to go straight back to town; he's guest of honour at a press dinner.'

'Make him change his mind. I'm not missing this opportunity to meet him. He could be very useful to us. It shouldn't be too difficult for you to manage, if he's as crazy about your sister as they say. He may be your future brother-in-law one day.'

'I shouldn't count on it.'

'Wanna bet?'

'You didn't pay up on our last bet.'

'But we agreed, darling, that it didn't count because the man went to jail.'

'*I* didn't agree. You're a filthy cheat. And I'm not going to bet about poor little Cynthia, and only a howling cad would suggest it.'

'The trouble is that in the first place you're jealous, and in the second that you don't understand the psychology of men like Nevinson. If he wants her, he'll get her. It's as simple as that.'

'What a romantic you are! And what about Edmund? Doesn't he count?'

'Not if he's in the way.'

'Darling, you ought to write plays for television. You've got just the right touch of *schadenfreude*.'

Later, when she was alone with Cynthia, this conversation came back to her with disagreeable overtones. Cynthia was very good about her trouble, very brave. She didn't show any of the anxiety she must have been feeling, though she was rather quieter than usual. No one guessed. And she wouldn't have them told.

Elspeth stayed talking for a long while in Cynthia's room, partly for the reason that Arnold was in a bad mood because Mark Nevinson had not stayed. Arnold of course blamed Elspeth for it, though it was really not her fault. It was Cynthia who had insisted that he must return at once.

Maybe if it had not been for her conversation earlier with Arnold, Elspeth could have asked her sister quite naturally: 'If anything *has* happened to poor Edmund, Cyn, will you marry Mark, do you think?' But now the question was impossible.

Monday morning, the guests departed. Cynthia stayed in bed. Arnold went up to town. Elspeth, having performed her household duties and exercised her daughter's horse, spent the afternoon gardening. At a quarter to six she returned to the house, kicked off her boots, dropped her gloves into a trug, switched on the telly for the news, and poured herself a drink. She sank down into a deep chair with it, stretched out her legs, and stared at the box in a stupor of fatigue.

Suddenly she uttered a loud cry and jumped to her feet. She ran to the door, shouting, 'Cynthia! Cynthia! Come *quickly*!'

'What's the matter?' came distantly from Cynthia's room.

'Hurry, hurry! It's Edmund!' Elspeth called, racing up the stairs. Cynthia came floating swiftly towards her, like an angel in a blue flowered nightdress. She looked, Elspeth noticed even at that moment, ravishingly frail and ethereal. She seized her by the hand and tore back down the stairs breathlessly. But they were too late. The man in the box was talking about a strike in Durham.

'It was Edmund,' Elspeth said. 'In Geneva. Shaking hands with President Whatsisname — '

'Are you sure?'

'Well, of course I am. It was Edmund. He's all right, darling. He's alive.'

Cynthia burst into tears.

★ ★ ★

Next morning, all the papers carried the photograph of Edmund with President Sadat and the Sheik of Saudi Arabia, the Sheik of Kuwait, and King Hussein, standing gravely posed, except for the little king who was grinning like a schoolboy. It was not considered hot enough news to be front-page stuff; in most papers it was rather depressingly tucked away. They also had a by-line or short paragraph (sometimes ironically enough on the same page as the report on the opening of the Middle East peace talks by the Rt. Hon. Edmund Burke, MP, Privy Councillor and Secretary of State for Mediterranean Affairs) about the nude body of a young woman found buried in the grounds of an empty house at Shippam Way in North Hampshire. The identity of the young woman was as yet not known. The cause of death was strangulation, and the police were treating it as foul play and were asking any member of the public who might have seen a car in that vicinity in the early hours of Sunday morning to notify the Hampshire police.

The sort of paragraph to be seen every day in the public prints, sad little notices of brutal crimes which passed almost unremarked among the mass violence in the rest of the news, or were noticed only by impoverished old pensioners eking out their empty afternoons by reading every printed word as an excuse to enjoy the free warmth of their local library. 'Nude

Woman Murdered' they read, and then their eyes move on to scan the small print beneath the titillating 'Angler Catches 20 lb Trout'.

No, no one would have noticed that commonplace item which was to have such far-reaching effects, because no one was looking out for it. Had McMurdo seen it, it wouldn't have meant anything to him — the body of an unnamed woman: he would have to be morbid indeed to connect it in his mind with Alys. Edmund did not see it because he was abroad and far too busy to do more than scan the parliamentary news when the daily papers arrived. And Percival never read the papers at all, regarding them as the waste product of a debased civilisation. Besides, it never occurred to him that there might be anything to look for. The woman had been buried where she would never be found. That had been the whole purpose of the exercise.

8

Horsham Division were the first to supply
Hampshire with information concerning
a suspect car from the general list of
stolen cars — the light green Cortina,
number BUF 888E, which had been
given a ticket for being parked in a
non-parking area between the hours of 2
and 6 p.m. The probability was that the
car had been stolen later that night as a
suitable vehicle for the robbery. Only, the
owner, or whoever had parked it in the
Horsham side street, had not reported its
disappearance, which was rather unusual.
If the owner for some reason didn't know
it had been stolen, the parking fine
would not be paid, for he would never
have received it. Given a few days' grace,
this provided a reasonable excuse for
pursuing inquiries about it to the owner.
BUF was a Brighton district registration
number. It was a new car, not difficult to
trace.

* ★ ★

The sandals Pauline Bury picked up in the copse by Torrington Common had not been found in the same place that little Philip Gurney alleged he had seen a dead woman, but some twenty yards away. Not too far though, in inspector Yapp's opinion, to prohibit the possibility of a connection between the two facts. The sandals had been lying a few feet away from a mossy ride broad enough to take a car, Yapp noted. He considered it possible that the dead woman and/or her murderer might have arrived up there by car, and from there he had transported the body to where he had concealed it in the heap of leaves. Twenty yards was a fair way to carry an inert corpse over rough ground while weaving through a belt of trees. Unless he was young and very strong, Yapp thought it more likely that he would have dragged her along by the armpits. That would explain how the sandals came to be left behind, dragged off passing over the uneven, root-twisted, bramble-tangled ground.

Monday morning, Yapp went up to town by the 8.50 to see the gentleman who had created the sandals. The interview was of the briefest. He had only one question to ask of him: For whom had he made the black sandals with the code number OED/AS/212818? The information was delivered within five minutes: They had been made for a Miss da Sylva of 26 Corunna Court, Wilbury Road, Hove, Sussex. Since it was still early, wanting some ten minutes to eleven o'clock, Yapp decided to pursue his inquiries back in Sussex, in the Hove quarter of Brighton.

*　*　*

There was still no word from Alys. For a full half hour after he had rushed from her apartment Sunday morning, McMurdo had meant never to see her again, had considered it to be *all over*; but as he sped back to London in his blue Lotus Elan, his wounded feelings underwent a change. He had been petulant and childish. He didn't own Alys. Alys

180

remained herself, a distinct and free person.

McMurdo determined to let the matter ride for a while and do nothing for a week. Then, if he had not heard from her first, to ring her casually. But poor besotted brute, he couldn't manage it. He hadn't realised to what an extent she had taken possession of him.

On reaching his flat, he went to the phone and dialled Alys's number. He let it ring while he walked about the room and brushed his suit and cleaned his shoes, but it rang in vain. Alys was still not back.

He tried again next morning, and allowed himself to try just once more in the evening. All the next day, anxiety was like a dull cloud over his mind. Although his thoughts ran restlessly in all directions, he never really thought she might be the victim of an accident, lying helpless and in pain in some hospital. No, he knew that nothing could have happened to her, because she had returned to Corunna Court and left her car in the garage. That much was evident.

Nevertheless by Wednesday he began to believe, spasmodically, that something must have happened to her, or where had she vanished to? Of course someone might have said to her: 'I'm off in the morning to Rome — or Outer Mongolia — why don't you come too?' just as he had said, 'I'm off to Jordan for a few days, how would you like to come with me?' and Alys would go with them in the same gay spirit she had gone with him.

Douglas persuaded a chum of his to ring the office and say he was not well enough to come in that day, and then raced down to Brighton in his Lotus Elan, bearing with him, as a charm against anger if she should be there, a dozen pink roses backed with graceful sprays of blue catmint and a jar of *pâté de foie gras*. It gave him, he hoped, an air of innocent goodwill.

The first thing he did on his arrival was to look in at the garage window. But the Cortina was still there, and his heart fell heavily at the sight of it, for its presence indicated that it was unlikely that Alys had returned.

The flat was as he had left it, even to the dirty whisky glass in the sink and the fishy plate which had held the relic of salmon. The last thread of hope that she might have returned to the flat sometime since Sunday morning vanished. It left him only with the obstinate desire to find out where she was. Without respect for her privacy, Douglas began sorting through the untidy clips of letters and bills scattered about her desktop, seeking some clue or hint as to her whereabouts. But there was nothing that seemed relevant. In the wastepaper basket he came upon his own enigmatic notes on the carrier bag and savagely tore into small pieces this evidence that he had been there waiting for her, and set the fragments alight. He then washed up the glass and plate and put them away: she should not know, if he could help it, that he had been hanging around there so patiently for hours.

What Douglas did find in the drawer of Alys's bureau was her passport. It was still in his hand when he went to answer the door. A constable in a peaked cap stood on the threshold. At the sight of him, McMurdo's heart seemed to leap up into his throat and perform a funny kind of tap dance there. At once he thought absurdly, *Something* has *happened to her, and he's come to tell me*, forgetting that he didn't live there and had no relationship with Alys.

'Yes?' he said, slipping the passport casually into his pocket.

'Does Miss da Sylva live here?'

'Yes.'

'May I speak to her, please?'

'I'm sorry, you can't. She's not at home.'

'When is she likely to be back?'

'I'm afraid I don't know. She's away somewhere.'

'You don't know where, I suppose?'

'No, I'm afraid I don't.'

The young constable looked perplexed. 'We've already called several times.'

'What did you want to see Miss da Sylva about? Perhaps I can help,' McMurdo said.

'Are you a relative?'

'No. But what's that got to do with it?'

'You live here?'

'No. Does that invalidate my information?'

'I just wondered how well you knew the lady.'

'You're not being impertinent, I hope.'

'No, sir.' He paused, took out his notebook, and cleared his throat. 'I understand that Miss da Sylva is the owner of a pale green Cortina, registration number BUF 888E.'

'Yes. So?'

'A car answering to that description is believed to have been involved in a felony.'

'You're joking! Are you suggesting Miss — '

'Oh no, sir. We take it that the car would probably have been stolen. Only, Miss da Sylva has apparently not reported its loss. Of course, if she's been away, that would account for it.'

'When is all this supposed to have happened?'

The constable referred again to his notebook. 'In the early hours of Sunday morning. The seventeenth, sir.'

185

'Ah,' said McMurdo, 'I rather thought it would be something of the sort. Someone has made a mistake. It couldn't have been Miss da Sylva's car, because it was here on Sunday morning. I saw it with my own eyes. I'd spent the night here.'

'I see, sir,' said the constable with a wooden expression. 'Do you happen to know where it is now?'

'In the garage.'

'Would it be possible for me to have a look at it? Just to check for the record.'

'I haven't a key to the garage, but you can see it through the window on your way out. It's number 26. Though I doubt if you'll be able to see the number plate.'

'Thank you, sir. Then if I may just trouble you for your name and address, in case we should need to get in touch with you, I'll not bother you any further.'

It had not been McMurdo's intention to mislead the constable when he averred that the Cortina had been at Corunna Court in the early hours of Sunday morning: to Douglas, 6 a.m. was early. Besides, it was obvious that it couldn't have been stolen or it wouldn't be in the garage now. It was hardly conceivable that a thief would return it himself even if he knew where it came from. So if the car *had* been involved in a felony, it seemed more probable that Alys was the culprit.

It was natural for Douglas to want to protect her. But he wished he had thought to ask what the felony was. It didn't sound like Alys, but she might have had too much to drink, and panicked. And then hidden the car in the garage and run away to some place where the police were unlikely to find her. *Poor little darling*, he thought on a wave of pity, and all this while he'd been imagining she'd thrown him over for some new lover. It brought tears to his eyes to think of it.

If his supposition was correct, then either she was hiding somewhere in the Brighton area, or she had gone off by train. Either way, since she had taken no luggage with her, she must be staying with friends, friends she could trust. Douglas found her address book and began methodically to go through it from the beginning. He intended to telephone each person in it, if necessary, on the pretext that he was Alys's agent and needed urgently to get in touch with her. It was a tedious task, saying the same thing over and over and getting no satisfaction, but he wouldn't give up. Sometimes to vary the monotony, he said he was from the BBC.

He was just thinking to himself that he would go off and have some lunch when again the doorbell rang. A tall man in a grey suit stood there, his left eyebrow twitched upward momentarily as though he had not expected to see McMurdo. But he only asked if Miss da Sylva was in. Douglas said she was not. The man then asked when she was likely to be back and Douglas said he didn't know.

'Do you expect her some time later today?'

'Miss da Sylva is away and I have no information as to when she will return.'

'I see.' But still the man hesitated, seeming reluctant to go.

'Are you a friend of hers?' asked Douglas.

'No,' said the man, smiling gently. 'Are you?'

'Obviously. Or I'd hardly be here, would I?'

'Oh, I can think of other possibilities. You might for instance have rented the flat from her. For a friend, you don't seem to know much about her, where she's gone or when she'll be back, and yet you appear to be in possession of her apartment.'

'That doesn't make me a burglar. I see no reason why I should tell a total stranger why I happen to be here or where Miss da Sylva is. I don't know who you are or what your business is with her.'

'I'm Detective Inspector Yapp of Regional Crime Squad,' he said, taking his warrant card from his pocket and holding it before McMurdo's eyes.

'Another one!' exclaimed McMurdo. 'What's going on? There's already been a policeman here this morning. If it's about the car, I can't tell you any more than I told him; that there must have been a mistake, because her car was in the garage at the time.'

189

'I think I'd better come in,' said Yapp, stepping inside. 'Is the car still in the garage?'

'Yes.'

'So Miss da Sylva didn't go to wherever she is by car.'

'Evidently not. It doesn't rule out the possibility of her having gone away in someone else's car, does it?'

'Perhaps you wouldn't mind telling me when you saw Miss da Sylva last?'

'A week ago yesterday,' Douglas said after a moment's thought.

'Was that when she went away?'

'I don't know.'

'She didn't mention it to you?'

'No, she didn't.' Douglas shot him a sideways glance, looked away, and then suddenly remarked in an offhand manner: 'As a matter of fact, I understood it was agreed that I should come down for the weekend. But not only was she not here when I arrived Saturday afternoon, she'd left no word for me.'

'So what did you do, Mr . . . You didn't tell me your name, I'm afraid.'

'McMurdo.' He frowned. 'What did I do? I waited, of course. Sat around, went to the cinema, came back. Actually fell asleep while I was waiting. When I woke, the garage which had been open — and empty — was closed. That was early Sunday morning. There didn't seem to be much point in waiting after that, so I went back to town.'

'And that was all.'

'Oh, I tried several times to find out if she was back, but there was never any answer.

'You weren't anxious?'

'I was furious and curious,' said Douglas with a smiling grimace, 'but not anxious. I mean I didn't imagine . . . ' The sentence trailed into nothing.

'You didn't feel obliged to make any inquiries?'

'I had no right to. It's nothing to do with me where she goes or with whom. She wouldn't thank me for making a fuss. Besides, why should I think anything's wrong when her car is here?'

Inspector Yapp, whose glance had been moving languidly about the room the while taking in everything, said: 'But still, you did come back. Why?'

'I came to see if her passport was here. It had just occurred to me that she might have gone abroad.'

'And did you find it?'

Douglas hesitated for a fraction of a second. 'No,' he said.

'So you think she may be abroad?'

'It would seem so.' He added sharply: 'You haven't told me yet why you're here.'

'Oh, I want to see Miss da Sylva in connection with a routine inquiry we're making.'

'I thought constables or sergeants did that sort of thing. Didn't you say you were a detective inspector?'

'I happened to be in the vicinity; it seemed a good opportunity.' He bestowed on the other his gentle smile. 'I'm quite a fan of Miss da Sylva's. She's a very attractive person.' He said apparently at random: 'Has she any relatives, do you know? A mother, a sister, anyone who might know where she is?'

'I know very little about her personal

life. I've only known her about two months.'

'Yet you have the key to her apartment. Do you think she gives her latchkey to everyone on so short an acquaintance?'

Douglas said haughtily: 'I've really no idea.'

'Time's getting on; I mustn't keep you. But I wonder if you could find me a photograph of Miss da Sylva before I go. I think it would be as well to circulate it to the police departments together with a written description.'

'Oh God, no, certainly not!' Douglas said quickly. 'Alys wouldn't like that at all; she'd be most annoyed. The very last thing she would want is any publicity of that kind. She'd never forgive me.'

'I wasn't proposing to make her disappearance public, I assure you. Only to make it possible for her to be found.'

'What do you mean, disappearance? Who said she'd disappeared? I never did. I said I didn't know where she was: I wish to God I hadn't said even that much now.' There was a frantic look in his eye.

'I appreciate that it's a personal matter

to you, Mr. McMurdo,' said Yapp. 'But it also happens that the police have their own reasons for wanting to contact Miss da Sylva. If you prefer not to be involved, I can get a photograph elsewhere. I only suggested it in order to save time.' He added mildly: 'Time can be of the essence on such occasions,' and left it at that.

McMurdo looked troubled and ill at ease. 'Do you think something's happened to her?'

'Don't you, Mr. McMurdo?' said the inspector.

★　★　★

That was how the Hampshire CID were enabled to identify the dead woman. Douglas McMurdo was brought down from London to confirm it. It was a terrible shock to him to learn that she had been murdered. He had seen more cadavers than he could count during his two years as foreign correspondent for a syndicated press bureau, but such experiences only deadened the springs of emotion; they did nothing to prepare one for a mortuary encounter with the corpse of someone one had known intimately.

He would have been even more shocked if he had known that he was their chief, indeed only, suspect. He seemed to have had the opportunity. He had admitted being in her flat on the Saturday and leaving it again early Sunday morning, which fitted in exactly with the alleged time of the murder; he could have taken the body away in her car and then brought the car back and concealed it in her garage, and after that returned to London in his own car. He certainly seemed to have no valid alibi for the time he was supposed to have been in Brighton. What did not seem to fit in with the story, however, was the episode which had undoubtedly taken place on Inspector Yapp's manor. Why should McMurdo have hidden the body there and then taken it away later to hide it elsewhere?

The police had not yet brought him in for questioning. They wanted first to trace the dead woman's husband and make further inquiries on several related matters before the inquest could be held.

Because he was the woman's husband after all, Hugh Daneforth too was asked to come down to Hampshire to identify his wife's remains, which he very reluctantly did.

Alys da Sylva's husband ran an Art Gallery in Cheshire. He was some fifteen years older than his wife, a quiet aesthetic gentleman, apparently totally absorbed in his highbrow work. One had the impression that it meant more to him than the death of his wife. They had been separated for five years. Still, one's wife . . . One would have expected some show of emotion, or if not that, at least a certain shocked grief. Especially for a life cut off so abruptly, so young.

Daneforth had met and married her when she was nineteen. He brought her to Manchester, where he lived at that time. They had lived there together for two years, and then one day she upped and left him. He had not seen her again. Shortly after that, he settled in Cheshire.

'I should have had more sense than to marry her,' he said. 'It wasn't fair to her. She was much too young to know her own mind. Even if I had been younger and she older, I doubt if it could have succeeded: we were temperamentally unsuited.'

'Why *did* you marry her?' he was asked.

'I hoped for something from her that it was not in her to give. I suppose I must have failed her in the same way.' And then to a further question: 'No, I've never wanted to marry again. There would be no question of a divorce. We're both Catholics. Alys would have felt just the same, I'm sure: it would be impossible for her to consider remarriage as long as I was alive.'

By a strange coincidence, he had been in Sussex at the time his wife died, staying at The Angel in Petworth. He had spent the weekend studying the famous collection of paintings belonging to the owner of Marchmont House with a view to persuading the owner to loan some of them to him for an exhibition. The owner had been absent at the time of his visit.

At the suggestion that he might have taken the opportunity to visit his wife while he was in the locality, Mr.

Daneforth was most indignant. 'I haven't seen or heard of her since the day she walked out,' he declared.

It seemed hardly credible, the inspector pointed out, when for twenty-six weeks of the year for the last two years she had been visible and audible for half an hour every Sunday evening to the greater part of the British Isles, not to mention numerous occasions on the radio. But Mr. Daneforth, with an extremely disdainful air, said that he took no interest in popular culture. He had no television, and used his radio only to listen to the news when it was important to have later information than the daily paper provided.

'We've got a right one there!' said the inspector to himself. 'There's nothing in his life that wouldn't bear a little investigation, I shouldn't wonder; all too lofty and innocent to be true.'

If his wife wouldn't consider remarriage as a possibility while he was alive, the same was equally valid for him: he couldn't remarry as long as she was alive. He had said he never wanted to marry again, but supposing he did? It was also worth bearing in mind the fact that Mrs. Daneforth must be a rather rich young woman. If she died intestate, which was quite possible with so young a person, who inherited? It would seem that she had no relatives except her husband. It might be useful to examine the finances of his art gallery. A provincial art gallery was hardly a lucrative business. Mr. Daneforth might be in need of money.

To say that one had spent the weekend looking at pictures was no kind of an alibi in a house the size of Marchmont. If his host was not there, who would know whether Mr. Daneforth was in the house or out of it? Easy enough to make an appointment, on some pretext or other, with his wife and meet her in some quiet country spot. Easy enough for him to find out his wife's address. Easy enough to get the key to her garage.

People as a rule made very bad criminals. They gave themselves hopelessly away. Which was just as well for the police. If villains weren't so stupid, they might never be caught.

9

Cynthia was at the airport to meet Edmund. He looked tired, but his face lit up when he saw her. He waved.

'How good of you to meet us,' he said, kissing her. 'We appreciate it, don't we, Martin?'

'We do indeed,' said his secretary.

'Listen, I've got to make a few quotable remarks to the press boys; they're waiting for me in the VIP room. I won't be five minutes. Why don't you fetch the car, and by the time you've brought it round, I'll be waiting for you outside the north entrance. Hang on to this, Martin,' he said, poking his dispatch case under Martin's arm, and walked away.

'You'd better give me that. You can't possibly manage any more; you look like a Christmas tree as it is.'

'Except that I'm not lit up,' Martin said, relinquishing it.

'Thanks so much.'

Martin Duke had been with Edmund for ten years. He was thirty-six, tall, slim, with thinning fair hair. He was hardworking, conscientious, reliable, and devoted to Edmund, who had this useful faculty of inspiring devotion in those he worked with.

'How was it in Geneva?' Cynthia asked as they walked towards the car park.

'Very nice, I suppose, but I never had time to see it. It was really pretty hard work, and the evenings were taken up with writing out reports on what had been said during the day.'

'How do you think it all went, Martin?'

'Extremely well, considering,' Martin said loyally. 'But Edmund's depressed, Cynthia. He won't say so, but he is. I know him so well.'

'Was any agreement reached at all?'

'Oh, it's early days yet,' Martin said cheerfully. 'We can't expect to advance very quickly. There are all kinds of seemingly insuperable difficulties. It's a bit like advancing through a minefield — one has to proceed with the utmost caution. But Edmund is a born diplomat and incredibly patient. He'll find a way to bring them together, if anyone can.'

'You really believe in Edmund, don't you?'

'Oh, absolutely.'

Edmund was not there waiting for them, of course, when they arrived at the north entrance, but he didn't keep them long. He came out of the building like a boy coming out of school, and Martin manoeuvred his long length into the back of the red Mini.

'Oh, it's nice to be back!' Edmund cried, climbing in beside his wife and slamming the door. 'What's the news? Tell me everything!'

Cynthia did not respond to his enjoinder. Her attention was occupied with taking the little car through the traffic and past the islands to the main gate. Only later, as they drove along the highway, did she mention quite casually that his bodyguard, Willie Thompson, was dead. Just like that.

'Willie? Good God, how did that happen?' Edmund exclaimed in consternation.

'A bomb. The poor chap was killed outright, luckily. It was meant for you, of course. The Bentley exploded into a sheet of flame.'

'My God! When was this?'

'Sunday.' She glanced at Edmund: he was as white as a sheet. She said: 'I thought it was you.'

'I wish it had been,' he said quickly. 'Poor old Willie!'

'For twenty-four hours I didn't know whether you were alive or dead,' she said reproachfully. 'I couldn't find out where you were. They said at the airport that you hadn't caught the plane.'

But Edmund wasn't listening. He said: 'He's left a widow and three children under six. What's going to happen to them now? He was so damned proud of those kids, you've no idea. I hope you went to the funeral, darling.'

'The funeral won't be until after the inquest,' said Cynthia.

'What a horrible business it is for that poor woman. You don't know how sick it makes me feel to think about it.'

'Then don't,' said his wife. 'I know it's

been a shock to you, but it's no good being sentimental about it, Ned. He didn't die *for* you but *because* of you. It was an accident, in fact. He wasn't meant to die, you were.'

'Let us not talk about it any more. What a wretched homecoming! The first thing I must do is to go and see Mrs. Thompson.'

'The *first* thing you must do is to see Detective Chief Inspector Walker of Scotland Yard. I promised him you would. I had to promise in order to stop him coming to the airport to meet you. For all I know, he'd have been standing at the foot of the plane waiting for you as if you were a criminal. I didn't think you'd like that. Not with the reporters and photographers there to greet you.'

'Well, thank you for that anyway. It's rather awful to think that poor chap would be alive now if you'd taken me to the airport as arranged.'

'Oh, thanks! There's no need to put the blame on me. If anyone's responsible, you are. If you hadn't lost Beau, I wouldn't have had to go down to Sussex to collect him.'

For a moment Edmund said nothing, and then: 'You got Beau back? I'm glad.'

'Yes, I got him back. You must tell me sometime how he came to be found wandering in a place called Torrington, over 60 miles away. I'd like to know.'

★   ★   ★

Walker said: 'I won't keep you long, sir. Just a few points to clear up. I understand from Mrs. Burke that there was some mix-up: you expected her to drive you to the airport and your wife had made a mistake in the time and found she couldn't take you. Wasn't that it?'

'That's right. I had to make other arrangements at the last minute. Thompson often chauffeured me to places where it would not have been convenient for him to arrive separately, and as he was to accompany me to the airport anyway, I asked him to drive me down. He was to pick up the car and meet me at the club after lunch. Of course he never came.'

'Did you try to contact him?' asked Walker.

'There was no way to do so. I knew my wife was out. No, we simply waited, my secretary and I, thinking something had detained him. We waited till it was no use waiting any longer, because we would already have missed the plane.'

'You did miss the plane, we know. It was this that led us to believe you'd been killed in your car.'

'We never went to Heathrow at all. It had been arranged that I would take an earlier flight than the one officially given out because of the possibility of an attempt on my life at the airport or, worse still, on the plane itself. You can see now there was good reason for the fear. It's pretty obvious, I think, that someone must have got wind of the change and altered their own plans in accord. They must have thought to avoid the risk of missing me by catching me in my own garage.' Edmund gave a short mirthless laugh. 'How chagrined they must have been to find they hadn't caught me after all, but only killed an innocent and harmless man.' He stared down at his hands.

After a moment, he said: 'I suppose one should be thankful it happened where it did, and not in the airport lounge or on the plane, when many more people might have lost their lives. It's always been a particular dread of mine that innocent people should be caught up in the machinery for my death,' he said in an undertone. 'That was why I didn't go to Heathrow and take a later flight. Instead I chartered a light plane from the Surrey/Kent Flying Club of Biggin Hill. My secretary booked the flight; and they had cleared customs and were ready for us when we got there.'

'So you knew nothing about Thompson's death when you left for Switzerland?'

'Nothing until my wife told me as we were driving home from the airport. Naturally I came to see you before I did anything else.' He shot a glance at the inspector and said with a rueful little grimace that he hoped all this would not have to come out at the inquest. It was no doubt improper to ask him to do what he could; nevertheless, he hoped the inspector understood that at this delicate juncture of the Middle East negotiations, any ugly publicity of this kind could bring the whole thing to a halt. The prime minister would not be pleased.

'I see your difficulty, sir,' said the chief inspector, eyeing him steadily. 'But it really is nothing to do with me; the inquest is under the jurisdiction of the coroner. Do you think you know who's responsible for the outrage, then?'

'I have no idea. On the face of it, it would appear to be an act of terrorism. And in this particular chapter of my life, terrorism simply means the Marxist Popular Front for the Liberation of Palestine. That is to say, a communist-instituted movement for the restitution of Palestine to the Arabs. To accomplish which end, any violent means is considered not only permissible but necessary and praiseworthy. They regard me as their especial enemy at this particular time because they know that if I'm able to persuade the Arab countries and Israel to come to terms by which they can live in peace, it will mean the absolute ruin of their aims. In consequence, it puts me at risk. Clearly they'd do anything to get rid of me.'

Walker looked up from his pad to say: 'And Mr. Thompson, as your bodyguard, would have been able to identify these people, I suppose.'

'He was able to keep his files pretty well up to date.'

'He might have seen and recognised his killer,' said Walker.

'However, I don't think we can take it for granted that it was the work of the PFLP, Inspector, just because they're the obvious suspects. There could be an equally fanatical bigot on the other side who might think it a clever move to commit an act of assassination in such a way that it would appear to have been perpetrated by their enemies. It might even — ' He hesitated and gave the other a long slow look. 'It might even, I suppose, be something to do with my private life. I don't think so, of course, but I don't *know*. And that's why I don't want it to come out just now and be blown up by the press into something tremendously sinister and create an enormous amount of bad feeling for no purpose.'

'Yes, I understand, Mr. Burke,' Walker said. 'I'll see what can be done.'

★   ★   ★

Horsham Police were surprised to receive payment of the £2 parking fine on the Cortina. That they had never expected in the circumstances. It came in a plain manila envelope, typed address, post-marked Rotherhithe, and inside were two pound notes and the parking ticket. It was, to say the least, *curious*. When Horsham had noticed the car number on the list of suspect vehicles, they had concluded that the car had been knocked off by some villain while it was still on their patch, the villain having pinched it presumably in order to use it for the robbery in Hampshire, in connection with which it was now on the stolen list.

But if that was so, who had paid the fine? It was hardly a thing a villain would do. Why would he? And it was equally unlikely to have been the car owner. Even supposing the car had been collected by the owner from Horsham and was only stolen later, why had the owner not reported the theft? The question was not only who had paid the fine, but why was it paid?

The envelope was passed to Hampshire CID, and thence to the assistant co-ordinator at Scotland Yard.

Now that the dead woman had been identified and the owner of car registration no. BUF 888E had been traced, it was known that the dead woman had been the owner of the Cortina which had received a parking fine on the day she met her death and later was stopped in Hampshire 'on sus'. The car was known to have turned round at that point and to have headed back in the direction from which it had come. Regional Crime Squad considered it probable that this was the car which had been taking the body of the dead woman to that vacant property in the hamlet of Shippam Way where she was buried. Which meant that she had been in the car when she encountered her murderer, or more probably murderers, since Constable Gamley had been quite definite that there were two men in the car when he stopped it.

The inquest on the dead woman was held on the same day that Edmund returned from Geneva. The report of it was in the papers next day. It was the first intimation Edmund had that Alys had been found. He had not had any anxiety about it — horror and hauntings, yes, but not anxiety — so certain was he that she would never be discovered. He no more thought of her corpse being exhumed than if she had been laid to rest in a coffin with all the panoply of a funeral and buried in a churchyard. It came as a heart-stopping shock to see the headline:

ALYS DA SYLVA
MURDERED
TOP TV PERSONALITY
FOUND DEAD

A verdict of murder by some person

or persons unknown was returned by the Hampshire County Coroner at today's Shippam inquest on Alys da Sylva, known to thousands as the winner of the last TV Personality of the Year Award.

Her nude body, wrapped in a rug and hidden in a shallow grave, was stated in evidence to have been found by Mr. A. Meyrick, a farmer, in the grounds of an empty house near Shippam Way.

The Home Office pathologist (Dr. Charles Grout) gave his opinion that Miss da Sylva had been strangled about 48 hours before the autopsy by a thin metal chain, probably part of a neck lace she had been wearing. Evidence of identification was given by the deceased woman's husband, Mr. Hugh Daneforth.

But it can't be, it can't be! thought Edmund. *What can have gone wrong? Percival said the place had been empty for years. He swore it couldn't have been sold, and he ought to know, since it*

213

belongs to his sister and brother-in-law. Oh my God, how frightful this is! What am I going to do?

He must have groaned aloud, because Cynthia said: 'What's the matter? Are you ill?'

'Ill? No, of course not.'

'You look ghastly. Are you sure you're all right?'

'Quite sure.' He wanted to say bitterly, 'Oh, don't be kind to me or I'll burst into tears!'

★   ★   ★

Someone else who read the item in a different paper also reacted differently. It was the name he recognised — *Mrs. Daneforth*. He remembered having heard it the previous Sunday when he had been server to Father Noone. The man had come in after mass and said he wanted prayers said for the repose of her soul. He was one of those bloody heathen Prots asking for prayers to be said for a Catholic person who had died without receiving Extreme Unction. Dennis was

214

sure it was the same name. Of course it could be a coincidence. And the man had said, hadn't he, that she had died the day before. Now how could he know that, Knockhouse asked himself with a sudden shiver of excitement, if she had only been found on the Monday?

He'd have to check times and dates and names before he took any steps, he told himself. It was the sort of information it was one's civic duty to take to the police. He saw his name in the papers; saw himself as a witness for the prosecution in court. His dull little eyes sparkled behind their spectacles at the prospect of delicious notoriety. The only thing was, if his name appeared in the papers, Old Noone would see it. Or if he didn't, some nosy old woman would see to it that Father Noone heard about it, all right. Now it was possible the good father would commend him for running with his tale to the police. But Knockhouse had a feeling that it was much more likely that he would bullyrag him to hell for taking it upon himself to reveal such matters without first asking permission to do so from his father in God.

But it wasn't as if he was betraying some secret of the confessional, now, was it? And the man was only a bloody Prot. And very likely a murderer. But if what the man said didn't count as being under the seal of the confessional, there was nothing to prevent Old Noone himself from toddling off to the police if he felt like it. Would he, though? And if Father Noone could, where was the harm in Dennis getting in first? Dennis had an idea that the police sometimes paid for information in cases of this kind. He looked down at his thin, shabby, grimy suit and ran a finger along the jacket's shiny edge. His clothes were so threadbare as to be hardly respectable. He didn't suppose the police paid much, not enough to buy him a new suit. But even thirty pieces of silver would be better than nothing.

★ ★ ★

The police did not have much to go on apart from the murdered woman's association with McMurdo. Him — and that rather odd gentleman, Mr. Hugh Daneforth. The lover and the husband. Of the two, McMurdo seemed the more promising suspect, and their 'inquiries' brought forth some interesting facts.

They learned that, besides being a journalist on the Nevinson press, he was Scottish nationalist, and known to be pro-Arab in the Arab-Israeli conflict. He had known Miss da Sylva a little over two months, and the week before she died they had spent five days together in Jordan and Lebanon. He admitted to having been in her flat on the day she was killed. Said he had spent the night there alone. Said he had not seen her. But he could have gone out with her in her car; could have killed her; driven her body across to Hampshire and there buried her, then driven back to Corunna Court, put the car away, and spent the rest of the night in her flat. He said he had left a note for her on the Saturday evening, but there was no trace of it. No sign that he had spent the night there. No one who remembered seeing him on the Saturday in this or that pub. No one who had noticed him at the cinema, nor had he a ticket stub to show he had been there. But he had been at Corunna Court; the porter going off duty had noticed the blue Lotus Elan in the forecourt because it was the only car there just then. Miss da Sylva's garage at that time was open and empty. Besides, McMurdo had the key of the flat. Had Miss da Sylva given it to him, or had he taken it from her after she was dead?

But there had to be reasonable motive for murder before one could say there was a case to be answered.

Of all this, poor Douglas knew nothing. He was too sunk in misery to be properly aware of what was going on around him.

He was at work in the Nevinson press building one afternoon, laboriously trying to apply his mind to the subject in hand, when one of the copy boys thrust a note at him as he rushed past. McMurdo opened it listlessly. On a sheet of un-headed paper, he read:

Dear Mr. Mac Murdo,

My very good friend Mansoor Saliba gave me your name and told me I should get in touch with you if ever I was in any difficulty.

For myself I would not trouble you, my dear sir, but I possess some very important information, I think of political significance. I wish only to tell it to you and you shall do with it whatever is right.

If you will be so very kind as to telephone on receipt of this — 323835, which is the number of the phone box down the street, I will be waiting there for your call. We can then arrange a meeting at a time and place convenient to yourself.

Yours very truly,
N. Shehab.

Douglas stared at this missive without interest. Wearily, purely because it was his job to follow up all such useless promises, he dialled the number given with the end of his pen and held the receiver to his ear. It passed vaguely through his mind to wonder if this Shehab fellow really did know Mansoor. Saliba's name was known to every Arab — as well-known as Georges Habash or Yasser Arafat. Probably he —

'Hub?' said a soft husky voice in his ear.

'Mr. Shehab?'

'Yes, Mr. McMurdo.'

'What do you want to see me about?'

'I would not wish to speak about it on the phone. I'm sorry. Only in private. Only when I see you face to face will I know if it is safe to confide this thing to you. You understand?'

'I should tell you, Mr. Shehab, that I think you have the wrong person. If you have information to sell, I can — '

'Oh no, Mr. McMurdo, please! The information is not for sale. It is worth much more than money.'

'I see. Where do you want us to meet? In a pub or café?'

'I think it is better that we should not

be seen together.'

Douglas said drily: 'Isn't that going to make it rather difficult for us to meet face to face then?'

'Oh no, Mr. McMurdo. I said we must not be seen together. I think it would be very suitable if I met you at your flat. I know where you live. If you will tell me what time is convenient, I will be there waiting for you. I shall enter the building and make my way to the fourth floor. In that way, no inquisitive person will know whom I am visiting. You understand?'

'I see you have it all worked out,' Douglas sighed. 'All right. I'll be there at 6.30,' he said, and rang off.

One thing was certain: this was something genuine. This fellow might not know Saliba personally, but he might very well be a member of Saliba's breakaway group from the PFLP. The whole carefully worked-out approach pointed to it. *All the same*, he thought, *I daresay it won't be anything that I can use.*

Naimeh Shehab came forward as the lift stopped and the doors opened. He was a slender man in his early twenties, with long lustrous handsome eyes and thick blue-black hair. His mouth was dark and full, the lips turned down at the corners; his face broad with a slightly receding chin. He was dressed in a fashionable but inexpensive suit.

'Mr. McMurdo?' he said in his soft husky voice. 'I am Naimeh Shehab.'

'Come in,' said Douglas, switching on the light inside his door. As the young man stepped through and the light fell on him, Douglas noticed that his rather handsome looks were spoiled by a skin curdled with old pockmarks. He looked intelligent, virile, energetic, but alas, as Douglas knew, such apparent qualities could suddenly turn to stupidity and inertia, no doubt due to malnutrition in childhood and inadequate education.

He was going to be told some stupid story, and the less interest Douglas showed in it, the more persistent and excitable and difficult to get rid of the man things would become. Already he was longing with quiet desperation to be alone, to sink down in the deepest chair with a glass in his hand and let the tears trickle out from behind his closed lids.

'Sit down, Shehab,' he said. He offered him a cigarette and began to ask him where he was from and how long he had been in Britain, and so on.

Shehab replied with bored civility but gradually began to show signs of impatience. 'Why is it that you English always have to know what education one has had and who one's grandparents were before you can believe one is telling the truth?'

'Firstly, I am not English but Scottish, and secondly, you come to me secretly with a promise of some important information and with no other bona fides but that Mansoor Saliba told you to come to me. I need to know a bit more about you than that if I'm to believe your story.'

'It is no story,' Shehab said fiercely, his eyes glowing. 'It is true. True veridical information.' He took out his wallet, removed a cutting, and passed it to Douglas.

It was a report of the inquest on Alys with a small smudgy unrecognisable photograph of her inset. Douglas stared at it in silence. It was so unexpected that he was quite taken aback.

'Why do you show me this?' he said at last.

'Because the information I have concerns the death of this woman.'

'Why come to me about it?'

'Mansoor said you were an important writer for the papers and also that you were sympathetic to Palestinian aims. I thought you would know what to do. I did not know anyone else who would help me.'

'And because she was a friend of mine?'

'I did not know that, sir.'

'Didn't you? The lady accompanied me when I visited your country a short time ago. There were pictures in your papers.'

'I didn't see them, Mr. McMurdo. I wasn't there. I have been here for five weeks. It was simply Fate that led me to you. If you were a friend of hers, I think you will want to know who killed her.'

'You think you know?'

'I do know. The murderer was not only seen but recognised, Mr. McMurdo.'

'By you?'

'Not by me, no. By a friend of mine, who I know is speaking the truth.'

'Why doesn't this friend of yours approach me himself?'

'Nothing will persuade him to do that. He is afraid.'

'What is he afraid of?'

'Trouble? Punishment? Revenge? Who knows?' Shehab gave him a prolonged enigmatic stare. 'If you cannot trust me, it is better that I go now before I say any more.'

'I'm quite willing to hear what you have to say, but I don't promise to do anything about it.'

Shehab put his hand in his pocket and then slowly held it out towards Douglas, palm uppermost. 'Have you ever seen that before?'

McMurdo recognised it at once. It was a black onyx crucifix about two and a half inches long, with the figure of Christ incised on it in silver. It was something Alys always wore; he had seen it often enough.

'How did you come by that?' he muttered.

'My friend picked it up after the murder. He handed it to me to show you as a token of good faith. The murderer strangled her with the chain from which this hung. My friend says it must have come away in his hand as he twisted the chain around her throat and then dropped on the ground.'

McMurdo said: 'How does your friend know that's what happened?'

'He was there.'

'You mean, he stood there and watched a woman being murdered?' he said, outraged.

'I did not say he was *near*, only that he was there. I do not think he could have seen what was happening, as the woman was killed inside the car. The murderer, leaning in through the window, would have blocked his view. Then the man went away — whistling as though he was calling for his dog, my friend said — and then, because the woman didn't move, my friend went up to the car and, behold, she was dead! He was very frightened. He saw this thing lying in the grass and he picked it up and ran away.'

'Ran away! Why didn't he go to the police? What kind of man was he?'

'He was afraid, Mr. McMurdo. Afraid that if he went to the police, they would say he had murdered her himself.'

'Why should they?'

'Because he is a 'filthy foreigner', Mr. McMurdo. He was right to run away, since it was nothing to do with him,' Shehab declared passionately. 'He is like me, an alien, only allowed here on short permit. That is why he would not come to you himself. He cannot afford to be mixed up in a murder affair while he is here. Don't you understand, Mr. McMurdo, we are known to be Saliba's men,' he said with a wild gesture.

'Why come to me now?'

'Because, my dear sir,' Shehab cried, 'it was not until the inquest the day before yesterday that my friend knew who she was, when he saw her likeness in the paper. Tell me, how could I come to you and say this man had been seen to commit a murder, when we did not know whom he had killed? We had no proof.'

'You haven't yet told me who you think

227

the murderer was.'

'Think! We *know* who killed her. Why else am I here?' Shehab said angrily.

'Don't get so excited, my dear chap,' said Douglas, pouring himself a scotch. 'Calm down and have a drink . . . Now then,' he said, handing it to him.

Shehab said sulkily: 'The man is Mr. Burke. The Mr. Burke who is your secretary of state for Mediterranean affairs.'

'Oh no! I don't believe it.'

'Why not?'

'It just seems a shade too pat, too convenient, that it should turn out to be the very man you want out of the way. It's true, isn't it?'

'Of course it's true. I am not afraid to say so. He is our enemy, he is being paid by American Jews to destroy us, we know that.' He banged his hands together impatiently. 'Do you think I would have bothered to come and tell you all this if the murderer had been anyone else?' He threw his hands into the air. 'What is it to me if some Englishwoman is killed? It's not my affair. Only because it is *him*, you understand.'

'How did your friend chance to be there when it happened?'

'He had been following him of course. He recognised him in a certain pub in Horsham. After my friend left, he chanced later to see him get into a car driven by a woman. Out of curiosity, my friend followed. He said Burke and this woman had lunch in a pub called The Wild Oat. My friend sat behind them. Then they went to this place among the trees, not the place where she was found later, but a place called Torrington. And that was where he killed her.'

McMurdo said: 'I don't quite see what you expect me to do about it.'

'You are a writer. People read what you say. And they would not do so if they did not believe that what you said was true. I want you to write about it in your paper. And then there will be a fuss about it.'

'There will indeed — I shall probably get the sack! I must tell you, Mr. Shehab, I don't feel at all inclined to take it on. If I did, I should certainly want to meet your friend first and question him personally.'

'My friend would not trust you not to reveal his identity to the police at some time. For the sake of our country and our cause, I have put myself into your hands. More than that we cannot do.' There was a silence. And then he said: 'Don't you think anything about the woman who was killed who you say was your friend?'

McMurdo's face became flushed and his eyes became very round and fierce and blue. He breathed heavily through his nose without replying; and then he turned away, picked up a pad and sat down.

'Tell it to me again, Shehab. Everything. From the beginning.'

10

Douglas had a sleepless night, trying to think what he could do with the information which had come to him so dubiously. Once or twice he turned on the light and sat up to read again the notes he had made on Shehab's story. As daylight slid between the edge of the curtains, Douglas fell briefly asleep and had a horrible dream about Alys as he had seen her for the last time in the mortuary, dead, but looking aged and withered; she was complaining that no one was doing anything to help her. He woke with a start.

From the office files he borrowed a photograph of Edmund Burke, and with the snapshot he had of Alys he drove down to The Wild Oat a mile outside Upper Cross, where according to Shehab they had lunched that Saturday. Before he committed himself to this business, he needed *some* confirmation of Shehab's story. The pretty golden-haired waitress remembered them without too much hesitation: remembered Alys because she had recognised her, remembered him because he had left a tip larger than she was accustomed to.

'Do you by any chance remember the dark man who sat at the next table, the one behind this man?'

'Sorry,' she said helplessly. 'Wait a minute — there *was* a dark-skinned gentleman at the next table. It's just come back to me. When you said 'dark', I thought you meant just ordinary dark, hair like, and that.'

As far as it went, then, Shehab's story could be true. The rest was up to him. Only, he still did not know how such a story could be handled. It came to him in a flash as he was driving back to town. He suddenly saw how he must write the article. It would have to be unmistakably about Burke himself, Privy Councillor and Secretary of State for Mediterranean Affairs, the Dr. Jekyll of the cabinet; comparing the benign and able public figure with the sensual and malevolent

Mr. Hyde of his private life. He would begin the article with a word for word description of the encounter of the man and woman in Horsham, as it had been told to him, and continue to the end of the story, leaving the two characters unnamed. And then from there jump to a snap profile of Burke's career, and so on. He'd call it *Dr. Jekyll and Burke & Hare*. That ought to do it!

Hallam, Douglas's editor, read it through several times. Then he called Douglas in.

'My dear good man, I can't publish this!'

'What's wrong with it? I've verified all my facts.'

'If we printed, this we'd have a bloody libel suit on our hands, man.'

'It was written with that in mind. The man's a murderer: he killed that woman.'

'You can't go round saying things like that, for Christ's sake! Are you out of your head, Doug?'

'No. There was a witness. He won't come forward himself, but I've checked his story as far as I can and it seems to be accurate. But the only way we can know for certain is by forcing Burke into the open. You've got to print it, Don. It's your bloody duty to make it public. If you don't, I'll take it elsewhere.'

'Give me time. I'll have to get a legal opinion on it.'

In fact, the opinion Hallam wanted was Lord Nevinson's — the Burkes were, after all friends of his. He took it to him in Park Lane. Nevinson read it through and glanced at Hallam over the top of his glasses. 'What's the problem?'

'Should we publish, sir?'

'Is it accurate?'

'I believe so.'

'This man ... McMurdo, is he reliable?

'I think so.'

'Do you want to print it or don't you?'

'It's obviously a pretty dramatic revelation. It's the sort of thing that *ought* to be made public. A tremendous story. It's also red hot and more than likely to land us in a big libel suit with the *possibility* of colossal damages. I wanted to know what you felt about it, sir, before I committed myself.'

'Honest Hallam, eh?' Nevinson gave his hearty laugh. 'It would appear to be a matter of public concern, but the decision is yours. You know I never interfere with my editors or tell them what they should or should not print. G'd evening.'

★ ★ ★

Mrs. Roffey, the Burkes' housckeeper, opened the front door to a scrawny young man in wire-framed spectacles and a grubby raincoat — not at all the sort of person one was accustomed to see on that doorstep. She regarded him with frigid disapprobation.

'Yes?' said Mrs. Roffey, frowning.

'I'd like to see Mr. Burke, please,' the person said with an ingratiating smile.

'Mr. Burke is not at home.' Mrs. Roffey began to close the door, and was stopped.

'Oh, isn't he? When will he be back, then?'

'I couldn't say.'

'I'll wait,' he announced. And to Mrs.

Roffey's surprise, he was through the half-open door before she realised it.

'Mr. Burke only sees people by appointment. You'd better write and state what you want to see him about.'

'It's a personal matter. He'll be glad to see me when he knows what I've come about,' the young man said with the aggressive effrontery of the downtrodden.

'Very well,' said Mrs. Roffey haughtily, and showed him into the small library. 'You can wait there.'

Knockhouse's hands were damp inside and he wiped them on his trousers as he sat down, and saw with horror that his nails were filthy. The man would think he was as common as dirt and kick him out. Well, he *couldn't*. He'd *have* to listen.

Knockhouse stared round the room critically. Professional habitude took him over to the Chippendale bookcase to see if they had anything of interest. His eyes scanned the shelves implacably. The Sitwells . . . rubbish! Iris Murdoch . . . tripe! C. P. Snow . . . finished! Somerset Maugham . . . worthless! Nothing there. Henry James . . . he was still sellable (he took one out, turned to the frontispiece and put it back). No good, it was a nice edition but dated too late. A set of *The Arabian Nights* illustrated by Edmund Dulac attracted him. He was looking at it when the door opened.

Cynthia said: 'Good afternoon. I'm Mrs. Burke. Who did you want to see?'

'Oh huh,' he said, turning. 'I'm waiting to see Mr. Burke. I was just taking a look at your books; I hope you don't mind. It's my trade, you see. I'm a book dealer. These are quite nicely got up,' he said, turning the volume between his hands. 'I'd give you a flyer for these if you wanted to sell.'

'But I don't want to,' said Cynthia with an astonished little laugh.

'No. If you ever did want to, I meant. There's nothing else of interest to me.' He set it back on the shelf.

'Did my husband ask you to call?' said Cynthia.

'No, he didn't actually.'

'I'm glad of that. I thought it might have slipped his memory. He won't be back till quite late, I'm afraid.'

'What d'you call late?'

'Nine or ten. Perhaps later. I think it would be better if you wrote to him. He does attend to all his letters himself, I promise you.'

'No, I can't do that. It's a personal matter, you see,' he said with the hopeless obstinacy of his kind.

'The best thing you can do, in that case, is to make an appointment. I'll give you the number where you can reach his secretary.'

'I've come all this way specially to see him,' he grumbled. 'He wouldn't be pleased to have missed me if he knew.'

'I'm sure he wouldn't. If you ring this number and tell the secretary your name — '

'Mr. Burke won't know my name. I've met him but he wouldn't know my name.'

'Oh, you've met him,' said Cynthia. 'When was that?'

'Last Sunday week, in the church of St. Peter and St. Paul in Welcome Street.'

'Really?' She smiled. 'Are you sure it was my husband?'

'I'm sure. He came to talk to Father

Noone after mass. I was there in the sacristy with him — with the father, I mean. Then the father sent me away because the man wanted to speak to him in private.' It had jumped into Knock-house's mind that he might serve himself better by telling his story to the woman. If she cared at all for her husband, she would be afraid for him and might well be more ready to cough up than the man.

Cynthia thought, *This man is talking absolute nonsense. What would Ned be doing in a Catholic church, for Christ's sake? He doesn't believe in religion.* She eyed the squalid little man with his sallow spotty face and greasy unwashed hair. He smelt repellently unclean. With an effort of imagination, it occurred to her that it might be difficult to make any sort of living out of secondhand books.

'He wanted to have prayers said for someone who had died,' Knockhouse resumed. 'A Mrs. Daneforth. Do you know her?'

'I don't think I do.'

'Mrs. Daneforth turned out to be Miss de Silver.' He looked at her with an innocent expression. 'You know who I mean: that woman who was murdered and was buried naked in someone's garden. You must have read about it.'

'I have rather a lot to see to; I must ask you to excuse me. If you'll leave your name and address, I'll see that my husband gets in touch with you.' Cynthia gave him a brief smile and laid her hand on the doorknob.

'But I can't do that,' he expostulated. 'I thought you understood. It's *important*. I daresay you're not paying any attention because you think I mean important to *me*, and so you don't think it matters. But what I meant was that it is important to Mr. Burke.'

'I'm sorry, what is it? Can you tell me?'

'I was trying to, but you weren't listening. That woman, Alice de Silver, who was found murdered last week — Mr. Burke wanted to have a mass said for her every year on the day of her death. That's what he told the priest. I didn't know who he was talking about; only later, when her body was discovered, I remembered. And then I wondered what

I ought to do about it.' He paused, and then added, 'Because Mr. Burke was asking for prayers to be said for her before anyone knew she was dead. *He* knew, and he knew *when* she'd died, but no one else did. You see what I mean?' He chewed his lower lip. 'I haven't got anything against Mr. Burke, but what I want to know is, ought I to go to the police?'

★　★　★

Ernest Bignall, the Member for Shropshire, came up to Edmund in the House and said, 'Look here, old man, if you haven't seen Nevinson's rag I think you ought to take a look at it.'

'Oh, ought I? Then I will,' Edmund said with his pleasant smile. 'What am I to look for?'

'You'll see it. Page three,' called Bignall as they were separated by a group of backbenchers making for the House of Commons bar. 'You can't miss it.'

Edmund found the paper. Bignall was right, there was no mistaking the article.

Edmund's lips compressed as he read; his eyes became cold, his expression grim. Someone spoke to him but he didn't even hear them. He went out on to the terrace and leaned on the balustrade, staring unseeingly at the boats passing to and fro.

It had *not* escaped Edmund's notice that the article about him was signed Douglas McMurdo. *I'm caught,* he thought, *like a fly on a flypaper. What the hell am I going to do? I can't see any way out. I'll have to take legal advice of course, but whatever Churnley says I'm in the cart, because everyone will expect me to sue and it'll look so damned odd if I don't.*

Churnley said: 'It's very serious. I don't see how you can ignore it. But what we can do about it is another matter. It might be possible to frighten them into settling out of court with a well-advertised apology; if we win, the damages will be colossal, plus the costs, and they just might prefer not to risk it.'

'You said *if* we win. Do you think we might lose?'

'Not a chance of it, my dear boy,' said

Churnley airily, waving his cigar. 'They've got about as much chance of winning £25,000 out of a single premium bond. Well, perhaps that's a slight exaggeration, but let's say it is extremely improbable, and they must know it. Or rather, they will once we've filed suit against them and they've consulted their lawyers. They'll quake, and if they've got any sense they'll give in.'

'It isn't quite as straightforward as that, Albert,' Edmund said. 'If it were, the paper would probably fire McMurdo and settle out of court as you suggest. But I don't believe that's what will happen. The paper is owned by Mark Nevinson.' Edmund looked at his solicitor, but to his relief the latter did not evade his glance. Edmund had the idea (true or false) that Cynthia's relationship with Nevinson was common knowledge in their circle. He said: 'Nevinson is in love with Cynthia. He wants to marry her.'

'And what has Cynthia to say about it?'

'Oh, she's enamoured of the ass. After all, the man is a multi-millionaire and I suppose few women can resist that lure.'

243

'Does she want to marry him?'

'God, yes. She wants me to let her divorce me, which puts me in a rather awkward position. I happen to love her. Though,' he added with a wry smile, 'not enough to let her go. Am I being a dog-in-the-manger, Albert? It's not only for myself and our marriage: I don't want Nicholas to be torn in two. How did we get on to this wretched subject? Oh yes, Nevinson. Well, you can understand how he must feel about me: you may imagine he doesn't exactly love my guts. *Anything* that would get me out of the way would just suit him. It wouldn't surprise me if he'd instigated McMurdo to write this piece. There's no point in being a millionaire if you can't buy what you want, is there?'

'If what you say is right, then there wouldn't seem to be much chance of it being settled out of court. We'll need to tackle it in some other way.' Churnley looked at his client casually. 'I suppose there's not a word of truth in this story?'

'Absolutely not.'

'Did you know this young woman?'

'I'd met her at someone's house, and I did take her out a couple of times.'

'Did you have a liaison with her?'

Edmund smiled faintly. 'Hardly a liaison, Albert. But I did sleep with her once or twice. I'm only human, and she was an extremely attractive young person. Anyone would have done the same; but there was nothing in it.'

'When was the last time you saw her?'

'Heavens, I don't remember! It must be months ago.'

'You didn't meet her either by chance or by arrangement on the day she's said to have been killed?'

'No.'

'You're positive about it, Edmund? Because the whole case is going to hang on that point, you know.'

'Absolutely certain. It was the day before I was leaving for the Geneva peace talks. I had a great deal to attend to before I left.'

'Naturally, naturally,' Churnley said absently. 'One wonders where the fellow got the idea from, that's all,' he muttered. 'He must have known it would be quite

easy for you to prove you were somewhere else at the relevant times.'

'But it doesn't have to be a fact for it to
harm me, does it? Once it's been said,
people are going to believe it. And even if
I'm able to prove that I could never have
done what I'm said to have done, because
I was somewhere else at the time, most
people aren't going to accept it as the
truth; they'll think the alibi is a cover-up
story that we've invented. Because the
mad majority always prefer to believe the
worst; it's more exciting,' Edmund said
with a kind of disdainful passion. 'It
seems to me, whichever way we handle it,
I'm done for,' he added gloomily.

'Oh, come now!' said Churnley. 'We're
not going to give in as easily as that, are
we? Just think of the damages you're
going to collect. You'll be a very rich man
— all untaxable too.'

'Ha! That's one way of being ruined.
I'll tell you something else, Albert. This
chap, McMurdo, was in love with Alys.
He wanted to marry her. She told me so
the last time we spoke.'

'You think that might be how he knew

about your little affair with her?'

'I asked her if she had told him about me. She said no. But I didn't quite believe she was speaking the truth even then. And if that doesn't seem reason enough for him to act with malice towards me, he's always been an enemy of mine politically. He hates everything I stand for, and to him I represent all he hates. I should think he's written two or three articles against me every year. I think, if I'm going to fight this thing, we could claim personal malice, couldn't we? He and Nevinson are out to ruin me. It's a deliberate plot. I mean the whole tenor of his article is so unnatural that it must be a trap.'

Churnley said cautiously: 'I don't think we can use that line of approach. We don't want to have to wash any more of our dirty linen in public than we need. That kind of thing does stick so in people's memories. Besides, if you don't intend to let Cynthia divorce you, you'll need to be very careful about your public admissions.'

'Yes, I will, won't I?'

'And just as careful not to bring out the

business of her affair with Nevinson, if you don't want to find yourself having to divorce her.'

Edmund thought this over in silence for a moment, and then he said: 'I rather fancy Nevinson would hate that story to be made public even more than I would.'

'We'll see, Edmund, we'll see. A libel action is not a game of revenge. Or at least, it's unwise to turn it into one,' said Churnley.

⋆   ⋆   ⋆

Geoffrey Scowen said gravely: 'This is a bad business, Edmund.'

'It is, Prime Minister.'

'You've taken advice, of course.'

'Oh yes.'

'Are you going to sue?'

'I don't see how it's to be avoided. How can one not bring suit for defamation when one is practically accused of having committed a murder? And yet the thing is so barbarous that it ought to be ignored. What would you do in my shoes, Geoffrey?'

248

'My dear chap,' said the prime minister, and he sighed. 'It is really a very ugly predicament. If you ignore it, people are going to think the worst.'

'Whichever line I take, I think I'm not going to be much use to you anymore, Geoffrey. Would you like me to apply for the stewardship of the manor of Norstead and rid you of a damned awkward encumbrance? Tell me honestly.'

'Certainly not, certainly not,' Scowen said hurriedly. 'I can't afford to lose you. Though I admit it couldn't have happened at a worse time.'

'But that's why they chose it. That's what it's all about. Didn't you realise that? They picked this moment deliberately, knowing that it would wreck the chance of peace in the Middle East. McMurdo, the chap who wrote the article, is in the pay of the Palestinian guerillas.'

Scowen looked interested. 'How do you know that?'

'I had the information from a reliable authority. I have no proof, of course.'

'It would be very useful if you could get

it. You must put someone onto it. With that in your pocket, you might succeed in turning the tables on him.'

Might? My God, Edmund thought, *doesn't he realise what it will mean if I lose? It's like being told you've got a fifty-fifty chance of pulling through a serious operation.*

Edmund smiled and said: 'I'm encouraged by your confidence in me, Prime Minister. I must say my constituents have rallied nobly to my support. I've had thousands of letters, and hardly one percent of them abusive. There's nothing like loyalty to give one a moral boost.'

'Nothing,' agreed Scowen, thinking how swiftly the most ardent partisanship could change to hatred and contempt. 'The best of luck, my dear fellow. We're all behind you, you know. Even the other side.'

★ ★ ★

It was an easy matter to trace the rug in which the corpse of the deceased had been wrapped: Liberty's label was sewn neatly into one corner. Two hundred and thirteen customers, it was found, had purchased rugs of this particular design from the shop in the last five years. Some of the customers were dead, some gone abroad. Of those who remained, Detective Chief Inspector Walker said: 'We'll try the London ones first.'

They were about halfway through the list of London customers when they reached Mrs. Edmund Burke. Mr. Burke was in when Walker called; he was just on his way to the House. Walker said he would not keep him a minute. Did he recognise this rug? Edmund said, Yes, it looked similar to one they had had. They had lost theirs a couple of weeks ago; it had been stolen from their car.

'Could you tell me where the theft occurred?' Walker asked.

'I'm sorry, I've no idea. Someone must have just lifted it out of the car, probably when my wife was shopping.'

It doesn't do to be too suspicious, Walker reproved himself. *It could be that he's speaking the truth.* At least he didn't deny ownership, which the evidence of the dog hairs made 99% certain, for they were just the same kind of hairs that a Pyrenean mountain dog had. Just to confirm it, Walker had removed a couple of loose hairs from the dog's coat for forensic to compare with those found on the rug, as he petted the great animal when it came up to greet him.

★   ★   ★

'Your boyfriend has got it in for me!' Edmund remarked drily as he passed the napkin-wrapped hot toast to his wife.

Cynthia glanced at him from beneath her lids. 'How, in particular?'

'Don't you read his papers? Haven't seen the article he published about me this week in the *Chronicle?* I'm rather glad. It wasn't very pleasant,' he said, carefully spreading a dab of Mrs. Roffey's home-made pâté on a corner of the toast.

'What did it say?'

'Do you really not know? I should have thought one of your friends would have been sure to see to it that you knew. Wait! I'll find it for you.' He left the room and returned shortly to place the opened paper on the table beside her plate.

It seemed to take her a long while to read it. At last she looked up at him soberly and asked him in a low voice what he was going to do.

'I shall sue him for publishing, and the writer of the article for writing, libel. There's nothing else I can do. They're attacking my public life through a lot of damnable falsehoods about my private life. I have to defend myself if I'm to survive. It's that cruel mixture of half-truths and lies that does so much damage.'

'But nothing you can do will eradicate them now. If you bring a libel action, you'll only nail them harder into the public memory. People seem always to remember the slanderous things that are said about someone.'

'What will they think if I *don't* bring an action, my dear? That I couldn't challenge these defamatory statements because they were true?'

Cynthia put her hand softly over his. 'Please be careful, Ned. I'm sure Mark can't have known anything about this, but he's a very tough character, and if you do bring an action he'll fight it.'

'I want him to. It wouldn't please me to have it settled out of court.'

'I mean, he'll try to dig up something that *is* true out of all that, to give the impression that it's all true.'

'I'm suddenly not hungry,' Edmund said, not taking the plate she held out to him.

'For goodness sake, make an effort. If you don't eat it, Mrs. Roffey will be offended.'

They exchanged a smile, and Edmund accepted the plate.

Cynthia said: 'I nearly forgot to tell you that someone is coming to see you this evening about 6.30.'

'Who?'

'He wouldn't give his name. He said it was important to you, a personal matter. Actually he came the other day, and I saw him.'

'Darling, you ought to know better than to make appointments for me with people who won't give their name or state their business. He's probably some half-crazed crank. Anyway, I shall be out.'

Cynthia said quietly, 'I think you should see him, Ned.'

'Do you? Why? What's he like?'

'A nasty little horror, but . . . ' She pulled a grimace, 'rather pathetic too. Called himself a dealer in secondhand books. He wouldn't tell me anything else about himself because, I suppose, he was scared I might set the police onto him.'

'The police!'

'I think he's trying to blackmail you, Ned,' Cynthia said.

'Me? Did he venture to say how?'

'He had some story about your having asked a priest to say prayers for someone who had died suddenly. Only, if I got it right, the point was that this someone had been murdered, and at the time you were supposed to have asked to have prayers said for this person, no one, according to him, yet knew the person was dead. Except you, he said. Which he seemed to think must mean that you were the murderer.' She shot a swift glance at him and said quickly: 'I'm sorry, darling, but you can understand why I said you'll have to see him.'

'What did you say to him?'

'Nothing. I said he'd have to talk to you, because I knew nothing about it.'

'Did you give him any money?'

'Of course not. Do you take me for a fool? I was brought up to believe one should never pay blackmailers.'

'A very sound precept.'

'What will you do?'

'I don't know. I'll have to find some way to stop his mouth. If your friend Nevinson got hold of it at this particular juncture, it would really . . . You won't mention it to him, will you, Cinzia? For old times' sake.'

'Are you mad? I should think you'd know me better than that, after all these years.'

He looked at her sadly. 'I know how you feel about him,' he said in a low voice. 'I ask you just to stand by me till all this is over. To show the world that you have faith in me. Afterwards it won't matter. I'll let you divorce me then, I swear.'

'Don't be so silly, Ned,' she said lightly. 'You know I'd never let you down.'

As a matter of fact, she was very angry with Mark, who she thought had behaved with a clumsy brutality she found offensive. She'd told him so. 'How could you let that spiteful article be published about Edmund? It's disgusting!' she had cried, storming in on him.

'Dear heart, what are you talking about?'

'You know what I'm talking about: the piece in the *Chronicle*. You'll have to withdraw it, Mark, and publish an apology.'

'Darling,' he said, smiling at her lovingly, 'don't deliver ultimatums to me, please. No one tells me what I have to do. Remember that, won't you, honey,' he said softly. 'What my editors choose to publish is their business. I don't interfere. If they consider that a piece of news should be published in the public interest, that's good enough for me. Friendship doesn't come into it. Publishing a newspaper is a public service and a very serious business.'

'Very serious when you malign innocent people.'

'Ah now, baby, you're the most loyal little kid in the world, but you don't understand that one can't mix friendship and truth when it comes to murder.'

'That is exactly what I do understand,' Cynthia said, pushing him away. 'And that's why I shan't see you again. Not while you're attacking my husband. Because when you hurt him, you hurt me and our son. Goodbye.'

'Goodbye then.'

It was their first real quarrel, the first time he had ever seen her angry. It amused and touched him to see her shooting off sparks like a Catherine wheel. But it had no effect upon his decisions. He hadn't got where he was by allowing himself to be influenced by a woman merely because he was in love with her. Nevinson kept his mind quite separate from his emotions.

11

The room was familiar to him now, and he assumed a posture of being quite at his ease, master of the situation. With a quite appalling jauntiness, Knockhouse said: 'Remember me, Mr. Burke?' and eyed his victim with a cynical smile, knowing the man would deny ever having seen him before. He was taken aback when the man admitted recognising him and had quickly to discard his next line of dialogue.

The man said: 'Of course you don't look quite the same; you were wearing a long black shirt with a sort of white petticoat over it, but I think you're the same person that I saw with the priest. What's your name?'

'You don't need to know my name.'

'As you please. Sit down and tell me what it is you want.'

'You could say it's about a problem I have. I'd like to have your advice,' said

Knockhouse, rattling off his prepared preamble. 'You see, I happened to overhear you telling Father Noone that you wanted to have masses said for someone who had died suddenly. A Mrs. Hugh Daneforth, you said, and you said she had died on the twenty-first. But then I happened to notice this lady's name in the paper about a week later where it said she'd been murdered; and they hadn't even found her body till the twenty-third. So, like, you were the only person who knew she was dead, and I didn't see how you could know unless, well, you'd had something to do with it.' He allowed himself a pause to give the man a chance to show some reaction. But the man said nothing, calmly listening. Knockhouse said: 'I don't want to get anyone into trouble. I mean why should I, what's in it for me? I never knew the lady, and for all I know she deserved to be murdered, it's not for me to say. But — '

'Just stick to the point, please. Your comments and assumptions are unnecessary and offensive.'

'Well then, that's all really. It's just a

question of whether I ought to go to the police,' said Knockhouse, leaning back in his chair.

'It's purely a matter for your conscience, I should have thought. Though I doubt that the police would give it serious consideration unless you had some kind of proof to offer.'

'Oh, there's proof all right,' said Knockhouse. 'It's all written down in the priest's notebook, dates and names and all. And if you're thinking to yourself that it's all right because you gave a false name, well, I knew who you were as soon as I saw you. I could identify you, and so could Father Noone if he had to.'

'You've come to me because you want money, is that? You're hoping that I shall pay you to keep silent. I'm afraid you're jumping to conclusions, in more ways than one. It doesn't by any means follow that because I happened to know that my friend was dead that I had murdered her or even that I knew she had been murdered. I could give you half a dozen possible explanations of how it occurred.'

'Oh, I daresay! I daresay people in your

261

position, who've had a proper education and all that, can wriggle their way out of anything, but — '

'Be quiet! What people in my position want to avoid is ugly rumours, however false they may be. I don't know what sort of money you had it in your mind to ask — ?'

'Well, I'm a fair-minded chap. I'd settle for a monkey.' He'd read somewhere that it didn't do to be too greedy in the first demand because it could frighten the victim into seeking the help of the very people he was most afraid of: the police. Knockhouse bore that in mind. He was thinking that if he could count on collecting £500 from him, say, every six months, why he'd have it made!

'That of course is quite unrealistic,' Mr. Burke said calmly. 'I wouldn't dream of such a thing, not for an instant. I'm prepared, however, to pay you a nominal sum on one condition.'

'What's that, then?'

'You'll bring me the priest's notebook intact.'

'You're joking! You want me to *steal*?

Don't you know that's a sin? I wouldn't do that, not likely. And then have to confess it to him afterwards. He'd slaughter me!' Knockhouse snorted. 'And what were you thinking of paying me for it?'

'Fifty pounds.'

'*Fifty pounds!*' Knockhouse jumped up in a rage of contempt, just as if someone had offered him 15p for a book marked 50p. 'I'd want twice that before I'd think about it, even.'

It had been a mistake to say so. Before he realised where he was, the man had pinned him down to it. He was to bring him the book the following evening at ten thirty. In the end, Knockhouse yielded because there was nothing else he could do.

In fact, Knockhouse went off quite pleased with himself: he'd never before had a hundred pounds all in one go. It wasn't as much as he'd hoped for but it was more than he'd expected. He walked home feeling for once that he was winning, and planning how the money was to be spent.

Edmund went for a stroll after lunch down to the famous Green Parrot Club in Soho owned by the Barnaby brothers, Babe and Big. Their gaming club had an immense clientele, and this was chiefly because of the special allure of those charming and notoriously wicked Barnaby boys. The service was of course high-class and generous, and there was the added advantage of other services which the Barnaby brothers somehow managed to provide for those in the know. The Barnaby brothers had a lot of friends. They liked to be helpful.

They were known to be villains, known to be behind all kinds of crimes, from drug-pushing to prostitution, but somehow the police were never able to pin anything on to them; they could always prove they were absolutely innocent. It had the effect of making them appear misjudged and persecuted. When clients commiserated with them after one of their periodic turnovers by the Jacks, Babe would reply: 'It's as I always say

— there's no justice, and that's the truth!'

No one seemed to know their real names; they were always called Babe and Big. Babe because he was the baby, and Big because he was the elder. They were devoted to each other and were never to be seen apart — like Siamese twins.

There were lots of reasons why the wicked should patronise the Green Parrot, but it was strange to see so many well-known people there, the titled and the respectable. One wondered how the Barnabys lured them in. Perhaps it was just that the innocent went because they hoped it would make them seem wicked.

Edmund had been introduced to the Barnaby brothers by another member of parliament. It sometimes amused him to take stuffy foreign visitors there. Besides, Edmund, who had an affection for the human race, did not exclude from it the Barnaby brothers. Once he had been able to do them some small favour, for which they had been genuinely grateful. 'Anything we can do for you, Mr. Burke, any time, you've only to say the word,' one of them murmured.

'Sorry, sir, the club's closed,' said the doorman this afternoon. 'Always closed for the holy hour,' he added with a wink.

'That's all right,' Edmund said. 'I've not come for the tables or the bar. I've come to see Mr. Barnaby privately.'

'Ah, very good, sir. What name shall I say?'

Edmund gave his name to the doorman to phone through. Babe came down to greet him and usher him up to their private quarters. 'Look who's come to see us, Big!' he cried, and Big jumped up, slamming shut the ledgers he'd been examining and thrusting them out of sight.

'Well, this is a pleasant surprise,' said Big, who was in fact a little man, smaller even than Edmund. 'And what will you take to drink, Mr. Burke?'

Edmund shook his head. 'Nothing; not during the holy hour.'

The brothers laughed at this sally.

'Ah, Mr. Burke,' said Babe, 'if we didn't have a holy hour stretching from three p.m. to seven I don't know how we'd ever keep the place open at all. And if it wasn't for a drink, what was it you came to see us about?'

'You said once that if there ever was anything you could do for me . . . '

'That's right. You have only to say the word and it's as good as done.'

'The first thing is, I don't want to have to come into it at all myself; I want to be unseen and unmentioned. All I'm asking you to do is to set it up for me. I want to have someone roughed up a little. Not badly, not seriously hurt, just frightened. If you know of a couple of long-haired yobbos who know how to handle little jobs of that kind, it would be very nice.'

'Sure we do. Nothing to it,' said Babe.

'You couldn't have anyone more reliable than Eddie and Louis,' said Big, looking at his brother.

Edmund said quickly: 'I don't want to know who they are, or anything about them.'

'Don't worry, Mr. Burke,' Big implored him. 'You won't know anything, they won't know anything, and we won't know anything. All they need to be told is who this character is and where he's to be picked up.'

'He can be picked up tomorrow between ten thirty and eleven, coming out of my house. No need to give them my name, just the address.'

'How will they know they've got the right chap?'

'Let's say he's not exactly the kind of person you'd expect to see coming out of a cabinet minister's house. He's a wretched little runt of a man with steel spectacles, like a fifth-rate clerk. They're to follow him; I don't want him jumped on anywhere near my home. He'll have a hundred pounds on him, which should be adequate payment for the job. I don't want them to take another penny from him though, please make that clear.'

The brothers held up their hands in horror, protesting against Mr. Burke paying for the job himself. 'There's no need for it, Mr. Burke. The boys will be only too happy to do it for us.'

'I think it's better we should be quite clear about this.' Edmund smiled. 'He'll have the money on him and they're bound to find it when they do him over. They'll take it off him anyway, so you might just as well make it plain to them beforehand that you know it's there.'

The brothers regarded him admiringly, saying one to the other: 'Do you hear that now! He's worked it all out like a pro.' And turning to Edmund, Babe added: 'They'll take it off him all right, Mr. Burke, and we'll see that you get it back, the whole bundle, untouched.'

'But I don't want it back. It's a payment. Do you understand? I simply want him turned over a bit for his own good.'

'It's got something to do with ethics, Babe,' explained his brother, adding, 'whatever they are!' He smiled at Edmund. 'We don't understand, Mr. Burke, because we've had no education. But it shall be the way you want it. Leave it to us.'

★ ★ ★

They came up on either side of him and caught him each by the arm. He turned his head to see who it was to the right of him, and took a handful of fives in the mush and another one in the belly. His breath came out in a groan and he doubled over. He was kicked to and fro like a football, caught by the jacket and flung from one to the other and received always with a punch in some extraordinarily tender place. Buffeted back and forth, he had no breath to groan or scream. Their hands grabbed at him as he reeled. And then he was lying on the paving stones and they were gone.

It was a long while before he could summon the will to get up. His glasses were gone, smashed. His face seemed to be full of blood; it came away wet and sticky on his hands. He felt ill and very frightened.

I'll never make it on foot, he thought, taking a few painful steps, clinging to the railings. Not a bloody Good Samaritan anywhere; like all the rest of the things they told you in the Bible, none of it ever happened. If he could only come across a taxi, for once in his life he'd take it, only there wasn't much likelihood of finding one in this part of the world. At the thought of the taxi, his hand went instinctively to his wallet, to the fat comforting bulge against his heart.

It wasn't there! It had *gone*! In a panic, he turned back and began to search the ground by the faint illumination of his lighter. When he found the splintered glass of his spectacles, he knew he was in the right place. But the wallet wasn't there. He wasn't really surprised. The deep pessimism that infected his life like a blight informed his mind as soon as he had marked its loss, that They had taken it, They had stolen his hundred pounds. They had known he had it on him and that was why They'd rolled him. The man had told Them to take it off him. He'd been *done*.

Eventually he reached his lodgings. Without even washing the blood from his face, Knockhouse flung himself on his bed and broke into bitter sobbing.

The loss of the hundred pounds was more agonising to him than all his bruised flesh. For a brief half hour he'd had riches in the palm of his hand, then had it cruelly snatched from him.

For days afterwards, the bitterness of it overwhelmed him every time he thought of it, and the sobbing would break out afresh.

Not having seen him in church and hearing that he was ill, Father Noone paid him a visit. But when he asked him what had happened, poor Knockhouse turned his face to the wall and wept.

⋆ ⋆ ⋆

'Martin,' said Edmund as he entered the room, 'you remember the day before we left for Geneva?'

'You mean, Saturday?'

'That's right. Do you remember what happened that day?'

Martin clipped some letters together which required Edmund's attention and set them on one side. He looked faintly puzzled.

'Nothing in particular that I can recall. Should I?'

'No, it was a perfectly ordinary day. But it is important that we remember accurately and in detail what we did that day, because we shall be questioned about it very closely. If Lord Nevinson and his crew are to win the case, their counsel is going to have to prove that my story is untrue. And you are the only one who can substantiate it for me, my only witness. I don't need to tell you that my whole future, my whole career, my whole life depend on my winning the action.'

'I know that,' said Martin in a low voice. 'And I hope you know that I'd do anything I can to help you. But I don't quite see what use — '

'Use! My dear fellow, without your support I can do nothing. I've just come from Churnley, with whom I've been discussing the case. He wants to see you tomorrow at two thirty. So I thought we should just go over the facts together to make sure they're quite clear in your mind. We're talking about Saturday the twenty-first of last month. There was a great deal of business to attend to because on the following day we were going off to the Geneva conference. Right?'

'Yes.'

'Right. I don't have to remind you that I spent the whole day here working with you until I left for my interview on *World Scene*, because that you can't have forgotten.' Edmund paused, and Martin looked up. Their eyes met.

'I see,' said Martin.

'Good. But it's not enough just to say that. We've got to be able to prove it. We've got to be able to remember every single thing we did throughout every minute of that day. It's got to be so firmly fixed in our minds that it will be impossible to shake us. What were we doing at three o'clock? What did we have for lunch and what time did we have it? Did anyone ring? Did either of us go out? These are the things we've got to remember, Martin, these and many more. All right?'

'Yes. I think I understand.'

'Of course, if you're asked anything to which you don't know the answer, you can only say that you don't remember. It's as simple as that. So let's begin at the time you arrived in the morning. It would

274

have been a little after nine thirty, I suppose . . . '

★ ★ ★

Percival not being on the telephone, Edmund had dropped him a line to say he would be in to see him the following day. The stocks had been sold to raise the money he had promised Percival. Edmund went to the bank to draw it out. He packed the notes into his dispatch case and came out of the bank.

Oh, what a fool he'd been! A man took what seemed at the time to be the right, the most practical, the only reasonable course, and found suddenly that he was in a bog, sinking fast and grabbing at every twig and tussock within reach as he sank.

But I'll get out somehow, he thought. *It's too absurd that a man like me should be in this predicament; it's like one of those nightmares from which one knows one could awaken if one could only find the right word . . .*

Yet all the while, unbeknown to

Edmund, the substance out of which nightmares are made was deepening. The man who tailed him to the old building overhanging the river at Rotherhithe supplied one more fragment to the jigsaw that was being assembled quietly and carefully at Scotland Yard. The assistant commissioner had had Edmund tailed continuously since McMurdo's article in the *Chronicle*. (By this time all the separate and disconnected pieces of the da Sylva case were being coordinated at the Yard.) There was one item in the da Sylva file which consisted only of the postmark 'Rotherhithe' taken from the envelope which had arrived at Horsham police station with the parking ticket and two pound notes. There was a chance, just a possibility, that the envelope posted from Rotherhithe might be from the person whom Mr. Burke had gone to visit in the converted warehouse there.

It wasn't difficult to find out the identity of the person who lived there. It was a man called Percival Leech, who had leased the old place for five years and usually spent a few months there each year. He was considered locally a bit of a mystery man, always going off to far off, little-known places, no one knew why, though it was said that he wrote books about his travels.

As it turned out, they knew more about him than that at the Yard. At least, the assistant commissioner did. P. Leech's high reputation as an explorer of ancient lands and their cultures, and his writings on the subject were considered very fine, perhaps too subtle and profound to be popular. The assistant commissioner admired his books very much and often turned to them when he could not sleep at night. Leech was also known to have done some good work in these outlandish countries during the war and the unsettled years which followed. He had not always behaved in a desirable way. Some of his behaviour had been decidedly suspect, in Nigeria for instance, at the time of the Biafran war; but then a great many people had felt strongly about that and the way the British government had acted in the matter.

It was Chief Inspector Walker who noticed an apparent resemblance in the plainclothes man's description of Leech and the Identikit version made up by P. C. Gamley. He thought it not without interest that Leech should be acquainted with the Rt. Hon. Mr. Burke, who it had now been alleged knew the deceased da Sylva and had been with her on the day she had met her death. Furthermore, the car Gamley had stopped that night was known to have belonged to the murdered woman, whose body had been concealed that same night within a reasonable driving distance from where P. C. Gamley had been assaulted — assaulted by the passenger of the Cortina driven by a man resembling the description of Percival Leech. For the first time in this awkward case, a chain of linked events appeared possible.

★ ★ ★

Cynthia made a point of being seen everywhere with Edmund on all possible public occasions, showing a radiant confident smile whenever the photographers were around. She was genuinely upset by this vicious attack on Edmund. It was dreadfully unfair. Her sense of loyalty was aroused and she was determined to stand by Edmund now and see him through this beastly business.

At the same time, she was dismayed to find that Mark had made no move towards her after her row with him. Not a word, not a letter, not a flower. He seemed to have dropped her. As though it was all over between them. She couldn't believe it possible after the raging passion he had shown for her. Even while she hated him, something inside Cynthia was pining for him.

When a week had passed, she learned with a sinking heart that he was cruising in the Mediterranean on his yacht *Ithaca*, crowded no doubt with slender sunburnt girls; or worse still, just one . . .

Yet the endless argument kept running round in her head like a tape recording: Why had he done this terrible thing to Edmund if it had not been because he wanted her? She hoped with all her heart that the judge would award Edmund socking great damages and costs. Oh, the hell with him, ratting out on her! He was King Rat. King Rat Nevinson.

12

Parliament was prorogued for the summer recess.

The schools broke up. Nicholas came home, was taken to see *The Mousetrap*, poked around in the latest antique supermarket looking for coins, ate in his favourite restaurants, spent a couple of mornings in the Imperial Science Museum, went up the GPO tower, had a larky day with some cousins bussing it round London, and altogether had a glorious whirl of pleasure after the rigorous discipline of school, before being packed off to Brittany to stay with the boy who had spent part of last summer's hols with Nicholas and his parents at their farmhouse in the Cotswolds. It was not desirable that Nicholas should be in England while the libel action was in progress. The boy knew nothing about it. But that happy state of affairs could hardly continue once the case was opened. The reporters would see to that, pouncing on him in the street to harry him with puzzling questions.

The case of Burke v. the *Chronicle* was tried in the court of Mr. Justice Kramer at the Royal Courts of Justice, Queen's Bench Division. Plaintiff, Mr. Edmund Burke. Defendants, the publishers and printers of the *Chronicle* and the author of the alleged defamatory libel uttered therein.

It was the plaintiff's case that the defendants had written, printed, and published certain statements about him which were untrue and defamatory, whereby the plaintiff had suffered grievous damage to his reputation. The defendants pleaded that the words complained of were true in substance and in fact.

The *Chronicle* article was allegedly about the plaintiff, at that time secretary of state for Mediterranean affairs, and was headed: *Dr. Jekyll and Burke & Hare*. The words complained of were: 'Alys da Sylva was last seen in the company of the Rt. Hon. gentleman. She was never seen alive again. Later when her body was discovered, it was found that she had been murdered. Would not one expect an innocent man to come forward and inform the police of when he had last seen her? The Rt. Hon. gentleman has not come forward.'

Sir Robert Frean, Q.C., for the plaintiff, rose, shifted his gown a little on his shoulders, and surveyed the court in solemn silence. Mr. Justice Kramer cleared his throat. 'My lord,' said Sir Robert with a slight inclination towards the bench, 'Ladies and gentlemen of the jury, *This is a very grave affair*,' and he paused. And then mildly, seriously, without the least hint of rhetoric in his tone, he informed the jury:

'A gentleman of the utmost probity, a servant of the crown, a privy councillor, a member of her majesty's government, with a distinguished record of service in war and in peace, has been scurrilously attacked in an article written, printed and published by the defendants. It is evident from the tenor of the entire article that its purpose was to destroy the plaintiff's good name and the honour and esteem in which he is held. The statements put out in this article are not only defamatory, they are completely false, and untrue in every respect. As I hope to establish to you very quickly.'

Sir Robert sat down briefly while his client went into the witness box and took the oath.

Counsel rose and said: 'Mr. Burke, where were you on the 21st of May?'

'At home. In Arundel Place, Westminster.'

'How long were you there?'

'Till about three o'clock. I was working.'

'Was there anyone else there?'

'My secretary.'

'Working with you?'

'Yes.'

'All the time?'

'Yes, naturally.'

'Is it customary for your secretary to work on a Saturday?'

'On occasion he does so, if there's great pressure of work. We were leaving next day for the Geneva peace talks. There was a great deal to be seen to.'

'So you were working from about — ?'

'About nine thirty. Till three.'

'What happened then?'

'My secretary left, and I went out. I had some shopping to do, and afterwards I took the dog for a walk in the park.'

'And then?'

'Then I came home. My wife was back by the time I returned. I went upstairs and changed and drove down to Wood Lane, where I had an appointment to appear in a programme called *World Scene*. That ended about six-thirty, as far as I remember. When I left there, I drove to Grosvenor Square to the American Embassy. I left there about half past eight.'

'And that's the record of how you passed the day on which it has been alleged that you'd driven down to Sussex to meet a woman.' Sir Robert glanced at the jury and sat down.

Mr. Howard Finn, counsel for the defendants, unfolded himself like a crane and made his leisurely way towards the box.

'Mr. Burke never works less hard than his employees.'

'Yes.'

'Did anyone see him arrive?'

'I don't know.'

'You don't know? Who opened the door to him?'

Edmund glanced thoughtfully at the roof and took his time.

'I did. I must have, because, as my wife reminded me, it was our housekeeper's weekend off.'

'Did your wife see him?'

'No, I don't believe so. My wife had already gone out.'

'Just the two of you alone in the house. And you're sure this was Saturday the twenty-first?'

'Quite sure. Because it was the following day that I left for Geneva, as I've already said.'

'And are you equally positive that it wasn't Friday the twentieth? Or Thursday the nineteenth? Or Wednesday the eighteenth?'

'Of course I am. On those days I was in the House.'

'I see,' said Mr. Finn. 'But no doubt during those five and a half hours in which you were working together, your telephone would have rung?'

'No doubt.'

'Several times, perhaps?'

'Very likely.'

'Can you remember who any of those callers were?'

'I'm afraid not.'

'Not one? Would that be because you did not speak to any of them yourself?'

'It would.'

'You left it to your secretary to deal with them. So we may expect him to be able to tell us the name of one person who might remember speaking to him at your house that day?'

'I think not. The telephone had not been switched through to my study deliberately, so that we should not be interrupted while we were working.'

One could not say there was an actual titter at this, but there was a kind of stirring in the court. For another half hour, Mr. Finn pursued his cross-examination, trying to break Edmund's story and getting nowhere.

Detective Chief Inspector Walker, at the back of the court, was thinking, *He's lying. Finn knows he's lying as well as I do. But he doesn't know about the dog; that the dog was lost for twenty-four hours.* Hadn't Mrs. Burke said she had to go down to Sussex to collect him, and that was why she couldn't take her husband to the airport? How was it that he hadn't seen the significance of that before? It had seemed so trivial that it had slipped his memory.

Edmund's secretary, Martin Duke, was called next. Sir Robert took him over the same points that had been made before through his examination-in-chief of Edmund. He began by asking him how long he had been Mr. Burke's secretary and went on to examine briefly the quality of their relationship.

'How did Mr. Burke treat you?'

'He has always been very kind to me, treating me like a friend.'

'Do you like working for him?'

'Very much.'

'Even though it often means working very hard?'

'Mr. Duke, have you ever known your employer to do anything unworthy or dishonest?'

'No, never.'

'Do you admire him?'

'Yes, I do, most certainly.'

'What is it you admire in him?'

Mr. Finn stood up to say plaintively, 'My lord, I must object to this line of questioning by my learned friend. He's using the witness as a character witness.'

Mr. Justice Kramer bent his head to gaze at him over the top of his glasses. 'I cannot see the objection to that, Mr. Finn. The witness has been in close association with the plaintiff for ten years; I should think he would be a person well-qualified to assay his character. Objection overruled.'

Sir Robert put the question again: 'What is it you admire in Mr. Burke?'

'I suppose, chiefly, his integrity.'

'Would you consider him to be capable of acting in the manner attributed to him in the article in the *Chronicle*?'

Martin said emphatically: 'Absolutely not.'

Sir Robert retired, and Mr. Finn arose.

'Do you consider yourself a truthful man, Mr. Duke?'

'I hope I am.'

'You realise that you're under oath.'

Martin flushed.

'Is it truthful to say Mr. Burke has never done anything unworthy or dishonest?'

'Sir Robert asked me if I had ever known him to do anything of that nature. And my answer was that I had not.'

'He doesn't lie?'

Martin looked around helplessly. 'Really, my lord, I don't see how I can be expected to answer Mr. Finn. There are occasions when any politician may have to lie.'

There was a muffled burst of laughter, quickly suppressed.

'I see your point,' said Mr. Justice Kramer. 'Mr. Finn, would you rephrase your question.'

'I withdraw it, my lord.' Mr. Finn had walked over to his junior, who handed him some papers. As he rustled through them, he said in a casual preoccupied voice: 'And where was the dog while you and Mr. Burke were working?'

'The dog?' Martin looked blank. 'I'm afraid I don't know.'

'You didn't see it?'

'No.'

'You were there over five hours. Did you never leave the study in all that time?'

'Not that I recall.'

'Not for lunch even?'

'Oh!' Martin put his hand to his forehead. 'I wasn't thinking. Yes, we went downstairs to the kitchen and had some beer and cheese.'

'In the kitchen?'

'Yes.'

'And you didn't see the dog?'

'I don't remember.'

'That's all,' said Mr. Finn in a high indifferent voice as he turned away.

'You may leave the witness box,' said Mr. Justice Kramer. 'The court will now adjourn for luncheon and will resume sitting at two o'clock.'

There was a rustle as the court rose in

deference to the judge, and then a clatter and a chatter as it quit the courtroom.

'I cannot do better, ladies and gentlemen of the jury,' began Mr. Finn in his opening speech, 'than to borrow from m'learned friend and esteemed colleague, Sir Robert — ' Here Mr. Finn bowed in his direction. ' — the very words he used to open the case: 'This is a very grave affair.' I go further. I say it is a very shocking affair, that a man holding one of the highest positions in our land should so degrade the dignity of his position, pervert justice, and bring dishonour upon his name.

'It is the contention of the plaintiffs counsel that the statements made about his client by the defendants are untrue in substance and in fact and constitute thereby a defamatory libel. Now, I have to ask you on this point, ladies and gentlemen of the jury, to consider very seriously whether you can conceive it possible that any newspaper would *dare* to publish the statements complained of, about a gentleman of the plaintiff's standing in the world, *if they were not true*. And I would ask you also to ask yourselves, for what *reason* would they publish such statements *if they were not true?'*

Mr. Finn, who had been leaning forward impressively, now straightened up and gave the jury a penetrating look. 'But — suppose the words *were* true! What then? If these facts came to the attention of the defendants, could they, could any responsible newspaper, ignore them? Could you, could any citizen, be justified in ignoring them, in turning aside and saying: 'It is none of my business'? But it is the business of a newspaper to see that the public is made aware of what is going on. Indeed it is more in the public interest that it should be informed of wickedness in high places than in the common everyday crime of the streets. Because if a man is in a position of trust, and is not to be trusted, then so much the worse for us if we don't know about it.' And so on and so forth.

Edmund watched the jury's faces as they listened to this oration. *He's impressing them*, he thought. 'How long can he go on like this?' he scribbled on a piece of paper and passed it to Sir Robert. 'Till the court rises,' wrote Sir Robert with a smile. 'But he won't want to risk sending his lordship to sleep. My guess is that he hopes to time it so that I shan't have a chance to cross-examine his witness today. Which means the jury will carry home with them whatever impression he wants to leave on their minds.' Edmund read these words and made a grimace. But Sir Robert shook his head with an imperturbable air.

Mr. Finn sat down at last and the defence's first, and indeed only, witness was called. He entered the box, looked darkly round with a bad-tempered expression on his face, and after some rather irritable expostulation took the Muslim form of the oath. He answered Mr. Finn's formal opening questions in a quick sullen patter: His name was Naimeh Shehab. Age 23. A Jordanian. Lodging at 24 Prince Henry Road, N.W.3. He was a student studying at the LSE. He had been to England twice before: last year for two months and a year at school when he was fifteen.

★   ★   ★

It had not been easy to get Shehab to court. First he had to be found. Then he had to be persuaded to say where his friend was to be found — the one whose story he had told that night to McMurdo. Which proved impossible. Shehab swore he had left the country.

'I don't believe he exists,' McMurdo declared.

Shehab had shrugged. 'Think what you like, my dear sir. It is of no importance to me.'

'That's where you're wrong. Because *I* think that information was yours, not your friend's; that *you* were the one who saw Burke and followed him, only you were afraid to say so.'

Shehab had smiled and said, 'Try and prove it.'

'I don't need to. You are the one who will have to prove it — in court. A subpoena will be served on you and you will have to appear in court.'

'And if I don't?'

'Then the officers of the court will come and fetch you.'

'And if I'm not here?'

'They will find you.'

'They cannot if I have returned to my own country.'

'Subpoena means 'under penalty', and if you fail to answer the summons, I promise you you will never be allowed to re-enter Britain.'

'Oh? Is that true?' Shehab had said uneasily, taking a sharper scrutiny at this untrustworthy slippery Englishman.

'Yes, it is. Don't be so tiresome, Shehab. This is a very important case with an enormous amount of money at stake, not to say several people's reputations. And all based on what you told me and what you in fact begged me to write. I did it for you. The least you can do is to do as much for me.'

'I owe you nothing,' Shehab had flung back. 'You did not pay me for the information.'

'You did not want to be paid. You said

296

that all you wanted was for the world to know about Burke. Well, I did my part, and now you funk doing yours.'

'You don't understand,' Shehab had muttered.

'Perhaps not. But do you think your people will? Will the Palestinians forgive you for chickening out on them? Or is it just that every man has his price?' McMurdo had shouted angrily.

Shehab's face had gone a curious greyish-yellow, his eye reddened.

'Well, think about it!' McMurdo said, slamming out. It was after all a question of McMurdo's skin or Shehab's; and McMurdo's skin was a damned sight more important to himself than that uninvited and uninviting Arab. He really didn't mind how he managed to persuade him, as long as the fellow turned up in the end.

★   ★   ★

'Mr. Shehab,' said Mr. Finn, 'will you cast your mind back to Saturday the twenty-first of July. What were you doing on that day?'

'Going down to Brighton . . . to see a friend. I stopped at a pub for a Coke and a sandwich.'

'Where was this?'

'A place called Horsham. There was a rather good-looking woman there. She was wearing a white frock and had on a chain with a cross hanging from it made of some black shiny stone. I kept my eye on her, but she didn't look my way. She was reading a paper. And then a man came in whom I recognised.'

'You knew him?'

'No, not personally, but by sight quite well. I had seen him many times in the papers and on the cinema and on television.'

'Can you see him in this court?'

'Yes, of course I can. He is down there, sitting next to the big man in the wig.'

'Do you know who he is?'

'Yes, of course I do. He is Mr. Burke, the secretary of state for Mediterranean affairs in the present government.'

'Did you know who he was, apart from recognizing him, when you saw him that day in Horsham?'

'Naturally, or it would not have meant anything to me.'

Mr. Finn signified that he should continue.

'I was annoyed to see him, and I finished my drink quickly and left. The woman had already gone. I was sorry for that. I drove off but found I was going in a wrong direction and had to turn back. And then I saw Mr. Burke again, walking with a big white dog, and they came up to a waiting car and he and the dog got in. The car drove away, and as it passed, I saw the driver was the woman I had noticed in the pub. I followed it.'

'Why?'

'It was going in my direction, towards Brighton.'

'How long did you follow them?'

'Oh, quite a while . . . till they stopped. Sometimes I lost them in the country lanes, but it wasn't hard to pick them up again; I was in a Mercedes and could go much faster than the other car.'

'So you were deliberately following them?'

'Yes. I was curious. I wanted to know

where the man was going and what he was up to.'

'Why should he have been 'up to' anything? Could he not have been simply going for a little drive with a friend?'

'I thought not. I did not think they were friends. They did not notice each other in the pub. Shall I go on? Well, they stopped at last among some trees beside a wide stretch of common land, a sort of heath.'

'Where were you at this time?'

'Twenty or thirty metres away. I had left the car on the road below and followed them up on foot. I waited a bit. It seemed to be the end of their journey, and there didn't seem much point in waiting any longer.'

'How could you have thought it was the end of their journey, when they had merely come to a halt in a quiet country spot? Was there a dwelling near?'

'Not that I could see.'

'Then what do you mean?'

'I mean that they had reached the purpose of their journey, a place where they could make love.'

'Did you see them make love?'

Shehab looked scornfully at counsel for the defence.

'I didn't see them *not* make love either. Tell me what else they could have been doing. The door opened presently and the dog got out and wandered away by itself. And then after a little while Mr. Burke got out. Then he came round to her side and put his head in at the window as if he had thought of something else to say to her. And then he went off in a hurry. I thought he would come back in a minute. But he didn't. I waited. And all the while, the woman never moved. Never moved at all.' Shehab took out a handkerchief and patted his forehead and his upper lip.

'She was too still for someone asleep. When people fall asleep sitting upright, their head goes this way and that,' Shehab said, lolling his head towards one shoulder and then the other to show what he meant, adding, 'because they are not quite comfortable. But this woman did not stir once. So I walked over to take a look. I saw immediately that she was dead.'

There was a moment's terrible silence in the courtroom after those words. Cynthia in the front row was white as death herself. From where she sat, she could only see the back of Edmund's head; she could not guess at his expression.

Mr. Finn, having milked the silence as if it was applause, said: 'Are you quite sure she was dead?'

Shehab said: 'I have seen too many dead people in my own country to possibly have been mistaken.'

'Did it seem to you that she had died a natural death?'

'It was not a natural death. She had been strangled with the chain she wore. It must have broken as he twisted it,' he said, clenching his fist and turning it in a horribly graphic gesture. Here Sir Robert intervened to object.

Mr. Justice Kramer said: 'Did you see the woman actually being murdered?'

'No, because his back was in the way.'

'Then you may not say so. Objection sustained.'

'I said it because the black cross was

lying on the ground just below the window where he dropped it.'

Sir Robert again objected.

Mr. Justice Kramer leaned forward earnestly. 'Did you see Mr. Burke drop the article you mentioned?'

'No. But I don't see how else it could have got there.'

'Mr. Shehab, if you didn't see Mr. Burke drop it, then you may not say you did. You're under oath. And you're not here to speculate about what you think may have happened. Objection sustained.'

The black cross was then passed up to Shehab for him to identify, which he did.

'And then,' said Mr. Finn, 'having found the woman dead, what did you do?'

'I was frightened. I picked up the cross and ran away. I was afraid that if I was seen there, I might be thought to have killed the woman myself.'

'Why did you take the cross with you?'

'It was . . . evidence.'

'What do you mean?'

'I don't know. It was just a feeling I had that it was important.'

'Was it your intention to hand it in to the police?'

'No. I was afraid they would not believe me.'

'Why should they not believe you?'

'Against Mr. Burke, your famous Minister!' Shehab was scornful. 'They would say that *I* had done it and was trying to throw the blame on Mr. Burke.'

'So you did nothing.'

'I waited to see what would happen. There was nothing else I could do as long as I could not say who the woman was. But when she was found and her photograph was in the papers, *then* I could say, 'I know who killed this woman.''

'Did you so say?'

'Yes, because I had felt very bad about running away. Eventually I went to Mr. McMurdo and told him everything.'

'Why did you go to him rather than the police?'

'Oh, my God, I have already explained about a million times that I was afraid of the police!'

Mr. Justice Kramer said: 'You must not

speak to the learned counsel in that manner. And while you are in my court, you will behave yourself and answer with due civility. Now. continue.'

'I went to Mr. McMurdo because I understood he was a friend of my people, and I thought if he knew all about it he would write about it in his paper and then it would all have to come out.'

Mr. Justice Kramer glanced across at the round-faced clock and said mildly: 'Mr. Finn, if you intend to carry the examination of this witness much further, I think it would be as well to stop at this point and adjourn until tomorrow.'

'With respect, my Lord, I have concluded my examination.'

Edmund remained stonily in his place beside Sir Robert as the courtroom emptied. Sir Robert said: 'They'll let us out the other way so as to avoid the reporters.'

Staring straight ahead, Edmund remarked: 'I'm done for.'

'Don't you believe it,' Sir Robert assured him. 'You're tired. What you need is a good stiff drink. The man is palpably a liar. I shall make mincemeat out of him tomorrow. Just remember that the battle is never lost until the last shot is fired.'

It's got nothing to do with the battle being lost or won, Edmund thought. I'm done for whichever way it goes . . . But I won't explain that to Sir Robert, as I don't want to discourage him from putting up the best fight he can. Because of course the dear fellow is perfectly right: whether I'm done for or not isn't the issue here; the important thing is for the battle to be won. The only real defeat is to give in. So pick yourself up off the floor and get on with the fight.

13

Cynthia was waiting at home when Edmund got back. To his surprise, she came up and kissed him. He could not recall when she had last done such a thing.

'My poor darling,' she murmured, her soft cheek against his. Edmund was so damned tired he felt he could simply not cope with an emotional scene just then. He patted her shoulder, smiled, and gently unlatched her arms.

'Poor old Ned, you do look whacked. And no wonder.'

'Let's not talk about it, darling, do you mind?' he said quickly.

'Of course not. Come and sit down and I'll get you a brandy and soda.'

Cynthia came and put the glass in his hand. She leaned down and loosened his tie for him. She said gently, 'It's going to be all right, darling. That dreadful man — '

'Please, not now, Cinzia,' he begged.

'No, I only want to say just one thing. It's something Sir Robert will have to be told; it's important.'

He steeled himself to listen.

★   ★   ★

Mr. Justice Kramer said: 'You will remember, Mr. Shehab, that you're still under oath.'

Sir Robert got up. With his profile turned to the witness box, he said casually: 'Mr. — ah — Shehab, how much were you paid to give evidence?'

Mr. Finn arose like a crow about to flap into the air: 'Objection!'

'Objection sustained. That was a most improper remark, Sir Robert.'

'I am obliged to your lordship,' said Sir Robert with a gratified air. He smiled at the angry young man in the box.

'Mr. Shehab, you have said that you are twenty-three years old. How is it that you are not in your own country fighting with your compatriots?'

'Because I am a student.'

'Ah yes, a student at the LSE, I think you said. What is the LSE? Can you tell me?' In a dulcet tone.'

'The LSE is the LSE. That is what it is called. I should think everyone would know.'

'But what does it *mean*, Mr. Shehab? What do the letters stand for?'

'I am not obliged to tell you.'

'You must answer the question, Mr. Shehab,' said Mr. Justice Kramer.

'I don't know what the letters mean, I have forgotten,' Shehab mumbled.

'The jury will hardly be surprised to hear that Mr. Shehab is not registered at the London School of Economics,' said Sir Robert with a smile.

'My lord,' said Mr. Finn plaintively, 'I really cannot see the point of this line of questioning. What bearing can it have on his testimony whether he is or is not a student at the LSE?'

'May I assure my learned friend that it has a considerable bearing on it. If your lordship will permit me my line of inquiry a little bit further . . . I am obliged to your lordship.' He turned to Shehab. 'In fact,

we should be maligning you, Mr. Shehab,
would we not, if we believed that you had
abandoned your country in its time of
need? You love your country, don't you?'

'Yes, I do.'

'You'd consider yourself a great
patriot?'

Shehab shrugged modestly.

'Or perhaps it would be more accurate
to say that you're against anyone who you
consider to be an enemy of your country,
even if they should be of the same race
and blood and nationality. In other words,
Mr. Shehab, you are a communist.'

'I am not communist,' Shehab sneered.
'I am a Marxist.'

'There's a difference?'

'I should hope so.'

'Well, we're obliged to you for pointing
it out, but we won't trouble you to
explain it. Is it not true to say you're here
as an agent of your party?'

'I don't understand the question.'

'Is it not true that you're here to carry
out the orders of your leader and his
party? Is it not true that you're over here
to destroy those persons who you

consider to be enemies of Palestine? Is it not true that you regard Mr. Burke as such a person, and that it's your aim to destroy him by whatever means you can? Is it not true that you were ordered to kill him?'

For a moment all seemed to be confusion and uproar, Mr. Finn protesting, the courtroom buzzing, and the usher calling sharply for silence.

Shehab moistened his lips. 'It is not true. None of it is true.'

Sir Robert turned away. 'I have finished with the witness.'

'Mr. Finn, do you wish to re-examine? No? The witness may stand down.'

Sir Robert then craved his lordship's permission to introduce another witness, some special evidence having come to his attention only last night.

'Who is it, Sir Robert?'

'The plaintiffs wife, my lord.'

Cynthia was duly sworn in and entered the witness box.

'Mrs. Burke, will you tell the court what you told me last night. I don't want to lead you.'

311

'Certainly, Sir Robert. I told you that when I was in this court yesterday I suddenly realised that I had seen the witness before. Mr. Shehab, I mean.'

'Can you remember when that was?'

'Yes. Very well. Because it was the twenty-second of July, the day my husband was flying to Geneva. He came up to me in my garage as I was getting into my car and said he'd been sent to fix Mr. Burke's car.'

'What was your reaction to that?'

'Oh, I believed him. He was dressed as a mechanic and he was carrying a tool case. Also my husband had told me he'd had trouble with the car the previous day, so it seemed quite natural that he should have it put right before he took it to the airport. I asked the man if he was taking it away and he said not if he could fix it there. Then I told him it had to be finished by one, and left him to it.'

'What happened then, Mrs. Burke?'

'I can't say of my own knowledge. But when I returned at about three p.m., a constable prevented me from entering the mews because, he said, there'd been a fire. It was in fact our garage which had caught fire. It was practically burnt out. I learned later from the police that an explosive charge had somehow been fixed to the ignition. The intention I am sure was to kill my husband. In fact it killed the man who was to drive him to the airport. The whole car went up in flames with a great bang, so I was told. They said the man must have been killed instantly.'

Someone in the court gasped, '*Oh!*' in horror, and was shushed.

Sir Robert said: 'You are in no doubt in your own mind that it was indeed Mr. Shehab who accosted you, posing as a mechanic?'

'No doubt at all. I believe him to be the man who was sent to kill my husband, but the plot misfired, and the wrong man died.'

After that, despite Mr. Finn's desperate efforts to save the situation, the result was a foregone conclusion, and no one was surprised when the jury found for the plaintiff. Mr. Justice Kramer elected to postpone the question of damages for forty-eight hours, as he wanted a little time to think about it. The court would re-convene at ten o'clock on Friday.

When the court broke up, Walker, who was keeping a sharp eye on Shehab, saw him push into a knot of people thronging the doors. Walker thrust after him into the crowd — the bunch of people with Shehab in their midst were being swept past the doors. 'No need to *shove*,' someone turned his head peevishly to complain.

Walker said: 'I'm sorry. I have to get out.'

'Well, that's what we're all trying to do, aren't we?' the man argued.

And in that brief moment when his eye was off him, Shehab vanished. When Walker reached the corridor, he was nowhere to be seen. *Oh, my God!* he thought, and ran to a telephone box. Seconds counted now. A general alert was to be put out immediately, especially at all ports and airports, for Naimeh Shehab, age 23, height 5ft. 6m, or 7m., registered as Jordanian, believed to be Palestinian Arab, wanted for questioning in regard to the murder of William Thompson in a bomb explosion on the 22nd of July. It was the best he could do.

The evening papers were full of the 'Dramatic Surprise Witness', as the banner ran on one paper, in the cabinet minister's libel action. Heaven knew that yesterday's unexpected turn of events had been exciting enough, but the latest development had added a glimpse into mysterious and extraordinary deeps. People who had thrilled yesterday to discover the depths of iniquity lurking beneath the sincere and fair-seeming face of that very genuine and earnest man, the secretary of state for Mediterranean affairs, were reluctant to admit that they could have been wrong. On the other hand, one had to admit that if it came to accepting the word of an Englishman against that of a foreigner, then one had to give it to the Englishman every time. Yet much remained inexplicable and puzzling.

'Of course,' said the know-alls, 'they had to hush it up. They couldn't afford to have it all made public, not when it's concerned with the government. You can bet your little cotton socks those chaps look after their own. They'll get rid of him quietly; he'll be given some safe and harmless job abroad and that'll be the end of it.' So they thought.

The person most disconcerted by all this was Detective Chief Inspector Walker. Yesterday everything had seemed absolutely clear. It all fitted together perfectly. And then Burke's wife got up and in a few simple phrases had scattered the whole thing to the winds. He didn't know where he was anymore. It made him tremble to think how close he had been to arresting Edmund Burke. If it had not been for the restraining influence of the assistant commissioner, who had advised him to wait another twenty-four hours, he, Henry Walker, might be standing there with egg all over his face, waiting to be charged with wrongful arrest. Nice! All the same, there were things he was not happy about, and they wouldn't let him rest. On top of which, he had let Shehab get away.

★　★　★

In The Fox, in Horsham, Mrs. Richards said emphatically: 'I don't care what you say, it doesn't alter the *facts*. I ask you, Colin,' she said, turning to the landlord, 'can you overlook the facts?'

'The only fact I can see, Manny darling, is that you've had a drop too much.'

'What's that got to do with it? What I'm saying is that what that Sheba man said in court yesterday was right. He was speaking with absolute accurcy. B'cause I know. I ought to have gone up there and test — and testi-fied for him.' No one was listening anymore. 'That's what I ought to 've done. Too late now. Case is over.' She sat down with a thump on to the bench beside a man and woman sitting silently over their beers.

'Excuse me for interrupting,' Mrs. Richards said, 'but what I was saying to my friends over there was that there's more in it than meets the eye. I'm not saying Sheba wasn't trying to frill him. Maybe he was and maybe he wasn't,' she said earnestly. 'What he said was nothing but the truth. The girl was here and he was here, cos I saw them. Saw the girl pick him up in her car. And the dog.'

'She's been going on about it the whole bloody evening,' said Colin as the couple gave him a look. 'I don't know why she don't go to the police about it and be done with it.' He was sick of the subject, and turned to serve someone else. But he had a soft spot for poor old Manny and he'd never seen her like this before.

She looked a bit stuck to the seat by closing-time. Colin got her to her feet and put an arm round her shoulders.

'Listen, Manny,' he said as he led her to the door, 'take my advice and you take your facts along to the police tomorrow morning. That's the best thing you can do. If they don't mean anything, then no harm's done; and if they do, well then, you've given a bit of a heave-up to British justice.'

'Ah,' she said, swaying a little in the fresh air, 'you're a good sort, Colin, a good sport . . . ' She stared vaguely down the road.

'Right then,' he said. 'Don't you forget now.'

He gave her a friendly little pat behind to set her on her way. What neither Colin nor any of them realised was that the reason why she kept on about it so boringly was that she could not bring herself to make up her mind about going to the police. She had an idea they would laugh at her. She had an idea that they looked down on her since her — accident.

The truth was that she hadn't been well enough to do anything about it before. And then yesterday it had all come out without her having to do anything, and she'd been greatly relieved — and just the teeniest bit disappointed. But today on the six o'clock news it had all been reversed. She couldn't understand it. For once, she had bothered to get an evening paper to try and make out what had actually happened. It was because it puzzled her so much that she kept arguing about it in The Fox, hoping that someone would explain it to her satisfactorily. But no one seemed to grasp her point. Their obtuseness defeated her. Or perhaps she was the one who was being stupid, she thought as her whirling bed became a cone into which she was drawn down . . .

She woke early, without her accustomed reluctance to face a new day. She made herself a cup of black coffee, painted on her face with care, and walked to the police station.

She gazed wistfully at the very young constable, so fresh-faced and innocent, who rose from his desk behind the counter to greet her. Young enough to be her son, she thought with a wincing nostalgia.

'I'm Mrs. Richards. I'd like to see Sergeant Trimble if he can spare me a minute. It's to do with that woman who was murdered some weeks back — Alys da Sylva.'

'If you'll just wait a moment, I'll see if he's free.'

★   ★   ★

'Well, Mrs. Richards,' said Trimble, ushering her into his office and shutting the door, 'nice to see you about again.

320

Feeling all right now?'

'Oh, quite all right,' she assured him brightly. 'I don't believe I've ever thanked you for what you did. You were very kind.'

'You won't do anything like that again, will you?'

'It was just an accident, you know. Silly of me to be so careless.'

'Well, you be more careful in future. Now, what's all this about Alys da Sylva?'

When she had told him, Sergeant Trimble asked her if she would mind waiting outside for a few minutes while he passed on the information. He got on to the Yard, stated his business, and was put through to Detective Chief Inspector Walker.

'Sergeant Trimble, Horsham Division. We did have some slight connection with the Alys da Sylva case, sir, if you remember. Her car was — '

'Yes, yes,' the voice on the other end said testily.

'Well, a woman has just come in who swears she saw Alys da Sylva on the day of her death in a pub here called The Fox. Also saw Mr. Burke in the pub, and later saw him and his dog get into the Cortina with Miss da Sylva in it. I thought you ought to know.'

'Think she's speaking the truth?'

'Oh yes, sir.'

'Why didn't the stupid woman come forward before?'

'She might never have come forward at all. Only she was upset the way the *Chronicle* action went yesterday, and she thought somebody ought to know Mr. Burke had been with the murdered woman earlier that day.'

'She could have said so a long time ago, couldn't she?'

Trimble said: 'Not really, sir. She's only been out of hospital a few days. Swallowed too many barbiturates on top of too much gin. Said it was an accident of course. But her boyfriend had let her down. So she was in no position to do anything about the case.'

'Doesn't sound a very reliable witness, but I'd like to see her,' said Walker. 'Can you get her up to the Yard this morning?'

'Do my best, sir,' said Trimble, and rang off.

The hunt was up for Shehab. Ports and airports were being watched, but it looked as though he had slipped through their fingers. From the moment he had walked out of the court, he had not been seen again. Shehab's evidence might no longer be acceptable in the case that was building up against Edmund Burke (that was where Mrs. Richards' testimony would be so serviceable, if it proved to be valid); but he was now wanted to answer to the charge of the murder of William Thompson on the 22nd of July.

* ★ ★

The day after Mrs. Richards went to the Yard, Detective Chief Inspector Walker and another plainclothes man stopped Edmund as he was leaving his house and invited him to the Yard. There he was formally arrested and charged with the murder of Alys Daneforth, otherwise known as Alys da Sylva, on the 21st of July, and warned that anything he said would be taken down to be used in evidence. Edmund said only, quite calmly: 'I never killed her.' Asked if he would care to make a statement, he said no, he would like to see his solicitor before making a statement. He was then taken down to the cells, where that evening he wrote to the prime minister, resigning his post in the cabinet and at the same time applying for the stewardship of the Chiltern hundreds, which released him from being a member of the House of Commons. His career was over. The next morning he was brought up before the magistrate and remanded to Brixton Prison.

They brought in Percival next 'to help us with our inquiries', and then asked him if he had any objection to appearing in an identity parade. 'Not in the least,' said Percival.

He stood in line with the other eleven men in the hall where the parade was to be held. And then the lights went out. Then someone came in with a torch and shone it in turn slowly from face to face. Once or twice one of the men would be asked to turn his face in profile. Percival was one of those asked. The man with the torch came back to Percival twice, then came closer, touched him on the shoulder, and all the lights came on again. And that was that.

★ ★ ★

Cynthia knew that Mark was back when she came home one day and found an enormous basket of the special pink orchids he always sent her. A little note tucked in among them said: *Dinner tonight? I'll pick you up at 7.30. Love.*

Fuming, Cynthia phoned through a message for Lord Nevinson that Mrs. Burke had a previous engagement this evening. She thought, *I never want to see him again.*

But instead of 7.30, Lord Nevinson turned up in Arundel Place at six o'clock. It was Cynthia herself who let him in.

'Oh honey!' he groaned, sweeping her into his arms and hugging her to him in a bear-like embrace. 'You don't know how I've missed you.'

He sat down with her on his knee and looked at her tenderly, gravely. 'Darling, it's so wonderful to be with you again.'

'Is it?'

'Didn't you miss me a little? Not even a little?'

'I lived.'

'Ah honey,' he said understandingly. 'You're still mad at me.'

'I thought I was. But I don't think I am anymore. It's over.' She got off his knee and walked away. 'I've had other things to think about.'

'Oh, baby, don't I know it. I can't begin to tell you how sorry I am about Edmund. It's a very bad business. That's why I so particularly wanted you to have dinner with me tonight, the very minute I got back, so that we could discuss the situation and decide what was to be done.'

'Oh! Not to go to bed with me?' Her eyes sparkled, wide and amused.

'Ah no, baby, please,' he said reproachfully. 'Don't be like that. You know if there's anything I can do, you have only to say.'

'You've already done it, my dear Mark.'

'Are you still on about the *Chronicle* business?'

'What do you think?'

'Listen, that was nothing to do with Edmund personally. You surely can't think I'd do a thing like that deliberately to ruin him?'

'Why not? It's all love and war, isn't it? You were determined to get me on your own terms, weren't you?'

'But can't you see, honey, that the beautiful thing between us has nothing to do with anything else? It is something special and perfect and apart.'

Cynthia said rudely: 'What bloody rot! Your sentimental rubbish sickens me. You tried to 'baby' me into accepting any nonsense from you. Well, I'm not a baby, I'm a woman. A married woman, what's more, who's not been behaving very well to her husband. Well, that's done with.'

'I thought you loved me.'

'So did I. Everything about you excited me, and when one is excited one gets so confused. And then I was bored with Edmund. But all that's changed now.

Perhaps it wouldn't have if you hadn't gone away just when you did. I don't say that out of malice, Mark; just to explain. I've discovered that I'm not like I thought I was. It's rather surprising, since one usually finds one is so much worse than one thought; but I've discovered something in me that I didn't know was there: loyalty.'

Mark said: 'That's cold comfort to go to bed with.'

'I daresay. But there are other things in life besides bed. If there aren't, then old age is going to be a pretty bleak affair. One runs half one's life by love, as though it was something terribly special and important. But suddenly it all seems like a child's game when it's matched against the realities of life. They're what matters in the end; not one's personal happiness. How absurdly narrow and trivial that seems to me now.' She smiled at him and held out her hand. 'So really, there's nothing more for us to say to each other. Goodbye, Mark.'

He stared at her. *He thought, I could win her over now, if I took her in my*

arms . . . *But I don't want to anymore.*
He got up and walked out.

14

Chiefly, Edmund seemed to worry about the boy, how he was bearing up under the notoriety of his father awaiting trial on a murder charge.

'Nicholas knows you're innocent,' Cynthia said. I told him so. It's not hard for a schoolboy to understand that a person can be wrongly accused. He knows it as a fact of history and a fact of everyday school life. You're his hero.'

'Poor little boy,' Edmund said. 'Have you done anything about Eton?'

'No. What do I have to do?'

'Obviously he can't go there now, at any rate not this term. If all turns out well, he can go there later. But for the next year, I think he should go to that school in Lausanne. Just for the sake of his health, mmm?'

Cynthia threaded her fingers tightly through his. 'It's going to be all right, Ned, honestly. But I'll fix up something in

Switzerland for him. Only, don't worry.'

'There's something to be said for jail: one really has nothing to worry about anymore.' Edmund laughed. 'But it does make the time pass hellishly slowly.'

'Time to make plans for the future.'

Edmund smiled at her. 'It's good of you to stick by me, old love. It means more to me at this moment than I can say. And just as soon as it's over, I'll set you free, so that you can marry Mark.'

'Oh, Mark! I said goodbye to him ages ago. It's all over and done with.'

'And you're not grieving?'

'Not over Mark, I promise you.'

Edmund said tentatively: 'Then it may be that something positive and real may come out of this nightmare in the end.'

★   ★   ★

The Crown v. Burke and Leech took place in the Central Criminal Court of the Old Bailey under Mr. Justice Overend.

The judge, in voluminous robe and wig, drew himself into the high chair on the dais, and settled himself. Below him were fitted, in a curiously orderly kind of disorder, desks, tables, benches, boxes, and in the middle a cumbersome wooden structure leading down to the cells below, called the dock. Burke and Leech, the accused, stood up within its walls, a warder on either side.

The charge was read out. Burke first. The clerk asked, 'Do you plead guilty or not guilty?'

Edmund Burke, in a clear but not loud voice, said, 'Not guilty.'

Then Percival Charles Leech was charged with being an accessory after the fact, and was asked what was his plea. He too said, 'Not guilty.'

The accused sat themselves with the warders behind them. The jurors were then called one by one and took their places in the jury box. In a few moments, all would be ready for Mr. Boas Q.C. to open the case for the prosecution.

He began by impressing upon the jury that they were to dismiss from their minds everything they had heard or read about this case. In particular, he asked them not to make any reference to or comparison with anything which might have occurred in a civil action brought by one of the accused not long ago. Nothing that took place there must affect this present trial. That case was over. The jurors were to remember that. The flaw in the prosecution's case was that they had lost the alleged eye witness to the murder, whose testimony had made him key witness in the other case. It was unfortunate that he was now wanted for murder himself. In any event, no one knew what had become of him. It was not known whether he had somehow succeeded in getting out of the country; his permit of residence had expired since some weeks.

The prosecution were obliged to do the best they could without him. They had the evidence of Mrs. Richards. They had the waitress and the wine-waiter from The Wild Oat. There was the evidence of the accused's Pyrenean mountain dog, given in the testimony of the man, Voicey, who had found it hanging about lost and unhappy on the road to Torrington. They had the evidence of the little boy, Philip Gurney, who had stumbled upon a dead and naked woman in a heap of dead leaves in the copse near Torrington Common on the afternoon of the day Alys Daneforth met her death. They had Detective Inspector Yapp's evidence of the sandals found by Pauline Bury in that same copse the following morning, which the prosecution would show belonged to Alys Daneforth.

It was the contention of the prosecution that Alys Daneforth was murdered in that wood sometime between two fifteen and three thirty. She was last seen alive when she left The Wild Oat in the company of the accused at approximately two p.m. Soon after four p.m., her Cortina was noted by the constable on the beat, parked near the Carfax in Horsham; half an hour later it was given a parking ticket for being in a restricted zone. Since Alys Daneforth was already dead, her car must have been removed to that place by another person; and that person, the prosecution contended, was the accused.

It was not denied that from there Edmund Burke had returned to London. There were millions of viewers who could testify to having seen and heard him giving a political interview 'live' that evening on a television programme called *World Scene*. Doubtless there were many people who could vouch for having seen him later at the American embassy. But from about eight thirty onwards, Edmund Burke was not seen in any of the places he customarily frequented.

He was not seen, in fact, until a quarter to two a.m. when the Cortina was stopped a mile or two inside the New Forest border. A traffic officer was stopping cars on that road for questioning in connection with a robbery that had occurred within the hour in one of the big houses in the district. The traffic officer became suspicious when the driver of the Cortina could neither produce his driving licence nor knew the number of the car he was driving. (The officer later identified Percival Leech as the driver.) The officer asked to see inside the boot. The man in the passenger seat handed him the keys and himself got out of the car and stood by him as the officer bent to open the boot.

The next thing the officer became aware of was lying on his back in the road, or rather on the grass verge. He had been knocked out, his two-way radio smashed, and the front-wheel tyre of his motorcycle slashed. It suggested that the boot of the Cortina contained something the men most particularly wished to keep hidden.

A little over twenty-four hours later, and barely twenty-five miles away, Mr. Andrew Meyrick, a farmer, found buried on a piece of land he had just purchased the naked body of a young woman wrapped in a tartan rug. The pathologist would relate that by the time he examined the body, it had been dead some forty-eight hours, more or less. The young woman was identified as Alys Daneforth. The rug in which her body had been wrapped belonged to the accused. The dog hairs which were clinging to both sides of the rug matched the type of hair from the Pyrenean mountain breed and proved identical to hairs taken from the Burkes' dog.

Alys Daneforth's body, though buried, was not outstretched at full length. It was curled up with the knees almost under the chin, as though it had been compressed into a small space and then rigor mortis had fixed its position. The body would just have fitted into the boot of a smallish car.

It was significant to the prosecution's case that the land in which the body had been buried had, up till the day that it came into the possession of Mr. Meyrick, been part of the estate of a couple by the name of Cahoon, who had been domiciled in the Bahamas for the last four years. For nearly six years, the Cahoon property had been on the market without finding a purchaser, except that seven acres of rough ground at the back had been sold to Mr. Meyrick in July. Before her marriage, Mrs. Cahoon's name had been Justine Leech — the sister of Percival Leech, who, it was the crown's contention, had aided Edmund Burke to conceal the body of Alys Daneforth.

The deceased had been strangled with the platinum chain belonging to the crucifix she wore. The crucifix had been wrenched or broken off, and was later found and identified as Alys Daneforth's. It was a rare piece of eighteenth-century Spanish work and had been given to her as an engagement present by her husband. The crucifix would be exhibited in evidence.

Apart from the sandals, nothing else belonging to her was found. Assuming that the sandals were inadvertently left behind, what was the motive for everything else having been removed? It was not suggested that it was a sexual crime or that the motive was robbery. The crown argued that the only reasonable supposition was that the body had been stripped of all its clothes and possessions to avoid recognition. Which suggested that it was feared if the body should be found and could be identified, it would point directly to the murderer. Which must mean that the murderer was someone with whom she was acquainted. The accused was such a person, and evidence would be brought to show that he had been on terms of some intimacy with the deceased for a period of several months before her death.

Means and opportunity were plain enough; perhaps the aforementioned intimacy provided the motive. The crown did not suggest that the crime was committed with malice aforethought. It was too obviously unconsidered to have been premeditated. Rather, must it have been a crime of impulse, perhaps of jealousy, anger or fear. But whatever the motive, it was a cruel and dastardly deed, everyone must agree.

It took two and a half days to examine the witnesses for the prosecution. It was then the turn of the defence. The argument which Mr. Gilbert Q.C., counsel for the defence, firmly put forward was, in the last resort, the total inadequacy and unreliability of circumstantial evidence. If A was seen to fire a revolver and a moment later B dropped down dead, that by itself did not prove that A had killed B. B might well have died from some other cause. Conversely, if B was found dead with a bullet in his heart and the bullet was found to have been fired from A's revolver, it did not prove that A had fired the revolver. In the same way, a man might be seen with a woman who later was found to have been murdered, without it necessarily meaning that it was the man who had murdered her. It was possible for a man to hide the body of someone he knew had been murdered simply because he feared he would be thought to have murdered the person himself. The tight circumstantial chain of evidence wrought by the prosecution did not add up to evidence of murder by the accused. It was only evidence of means and opportunity. No motive had been found because no motive could be found. There was no earthly reason why Edmund Burke should have killed Alys Daneforth.

It was lucky for the defence and lucky for Edmund that all the evidence of the civil case was annulled here. It would not be brought against him in this place that he had committed perjury before, nor would it be argued now that his present statements were not to be trusted because he had lied before. Nor could Shehab's testimony of having seen him kill Alys be brought against him. It meant that he could put forward a quite different line of pleading. He could, in fact, tell the truth. Though whether he would be believed remained to be seen.

Edmund Burke was called to give evidence in his own defence. He took the oath, entered the witness box, and said that he had met Alys da Sylva (as he had known her) by pre-arrangement at Horsham on the 21st of July. She had rung him to say she had something important to communicate to him before he went away; and so he had agreed to meet her, though the time was inopportune.

Mr. Gilbert said: 'If the time was inopportune, why did you agree to meet her, Mr. Burke?'

'I knew it must be important because it was the first time she had ever rung me at home. Additionally, she was a young woman who had a wide and heterogeneous acquaintance and in consequence often came by all kinds of useful information which she would pass on to me. Since she so particularly wanted to tell me whatever it was *before* I left for the Geneva talks, I took it to mean that it was concerned with the peace talks. That was why I agreed to meet her.'

'The prosecution has implied that there must have been some sinister reason behind your meeting her in this oddly furtive manner. Why was it that you pretended not to recognise each other at The Fox?'

'Because of her many television appearances and her great popularity, Alys was known by sight to literally millions of people in the British Isles; and as a privy councillor I had to be discreet. If we were seen together and recognized, it could have made it very awkward.'

'You mean, because people would have jumped to the conclusion that you were having an affair?'

'No, although that would have been an embarrassment for me. But in this age of violence in which we live, it would have meant putting Alys at risk. If, for instance, it had come to the ears of those among her acquaintances from whom she was passing information to me. I cannot say more than that. I must beg for the discretion of the court,' Edmund said, looking towards his lordship.

The judge said that at this juncture he had no wish to hear evidence in camera unless it became absolutely necessary.

The accused continued. He related how they had become aware that they were being followed by a black Mercedes. This was unexpected, and it made him nervous. For a while he had wondered uneasily if Alys da Sylva was setting something up for him. She managed — as he thought — to shake the car off their tracks. After lunching at The Wild Oat at the suggestion of Miss da Sylva, he had suggested taking the dog for a country walk. But Miss da Sylva said she had only the sandals she was wearing, which were quite unsuitable. But she drove to a quiet spot, and for a while he sat there in the car with her while she told him what it was she had wanted to see him about. (Here Mr. Burke, in answer to Mr. Gilbert's question, said that he was not able to disclose the subject of their conversation, beyond the fact that she had warned him urgently of the danger she believed him to be in from the Palestinian terrorists, about which she had recently acquired direct information while she was in the Middle East.)

Meanwhile, the dog had become restless and he had let it out by itself. Shortly afterwards, he got out to take the dog for its walk and was alarmed to find that it was nowhere to be seen. The dog belonged to his wife, who was devoted to it, and he knew how upset she would be if it was lost. He set off across the common, calling and whistling for it. But in vain.

He must have been gone nearly half an hour. When he got back to the car, it was to find that Alys was dead, and it appeared to him obvious that she had been murdered.

'What was your reaction to that, Mr. Burke?'

'Extreme consternation. I was utterly dismayed. Apart from my personal feelings in the matter, I felt as if I was caught in a trap. It was too much of a

344

coincidence for her to have been murdered by chance. It seemed to me her death must be connected with me; it must be meant to involve me somehow. But in the turmoil of my mind, I couldn't see how. I could only think of its effect upon the prospect of my forthcoming attempts to find terms of agreement between Israel and the United Arab Republics. I believed then, and I still am of the opinion now, that if the situation is not resolved soon, it may escalate into a third major war.'

'Why did you not go straight to the police, Mr. Burke?' Mr. Gilbert inquired.

'I wanted to, believe me. But if once it was known that Alys da Sylva had been murdered, it would be made to look as though it was because of something she had told me about the Middle East situation. And gone at one stroke would be the very basis of trust and impartiality on which my chance of success relied.

'I sat there in the car beside her, trying to think what I should do. I had very little time in which to make up my mind. The choice was between doing the obviously right thing according to the social conventions in which I was brought up and doing what seemed to me best in the situation as it was. Faced with it in that way, it seemed to me it would have been shameful to do the trivial and expected thing without regard to the consequences. I made the harder choice and decided to conceal her death.'

'Knowing it to be murder?'

'Knowing it to be murder,' Edmund agreed. 'Knowing too that the laws of society must be observed if that society is to survive, and those laws must always be to protect its citizens, and therefore the murderer must be caught and dealt with according to the custom of the day. I saw this instance as one of those exceptions which prove the rule.'

'I should like at this point,' said Mr. Gilbert, 'to ask if you formed any impression of how the murderer could have strangled Miss da Sylva with her neck-chain while she was seated inside the car?'

'I should explain that I had no knowledge at the time of how she had been strangled. I was in the same position as everyone else; it was only later that I learned her own neck-chain had been used. Naturally I've thought about it a great deal. It seemed to me it wouldn't make much difference whether the murderer was known to her or not — always providing it wasn't someone of whom she was afraid. It would be quite easy for someone to come up to the open window and ask if she had a light for his cigarette, say. He could lean in with the cigarette in his mouth, and as she looked for her matches or lighter, he had only to seize the chain by the cross and twist it quickly behind her head. She'd have no time to struggle or cry out. It would be all over in a minute. I should like to point out that her bag was open in her lap and some of the contents had spilled out, which makes it, I think, a probable explanation.'

It was the end of the first day. Edmund Burke had been in the witness box for six hours. He looked tired but calm as he vanished down the steps from the dock.

★　★　★

Mr. Gilbert started him off the next morning with a question. 'Having decided to conceal Miss da Sylva's death, what steps did you take?'

'I had to look for a suitable place where the body could be hidden, for a time anyway. Not far away there was a hollow place between three trees, full of dead leaves. I thought it would do. It was a dreadful business having to transport her there.' For the first time he faltered.

Mr. Gilbert said: 'Did you transport her there just as she was?'

'I think that was when her sandals fell off. I'd forgotten to remove them when I removed the rest of her things.'

'Why did you do that, Mr. Burke?'

'It was with great reluctance . . . It seemed a terrible indignity . . . '

The judge asked him to speak up. Mr. Burke apologised and raised his head again, looking very pale.

'Like the sandals, everything Alys wore was handmade. It meant it was terribly easy to trace. It seemed quite absurd to go to the lengths of hiding the body, and yet leaving it to be easily identified if it should be found before I could arrange somewhere better for her. I wrapped her in a rug and covered her with leaves. Then I drove her car back to Horsham and picked up my own.'

'What happened after you left the American embassy?'

'I went to see Mr. Leech. He was the only person I could think of whom I could trust. The only person I knew who was unquestioningly fearless and true and straight, and who had never lived by the rules. He's a man I admire very much.'

'You've known him a long time?'

'Nearly forty years. I've never known him to do anything underhanded or mean. I told him some part of this story, and as I expected and hoped, he offered to help me. I had to have someone to drive the second car. If he'd done just that, it would have been enough; but being the man he is, he insisted on taking part in the whole affair.'

Edmund paused. 'There's not much more to tell. We drove in my car to Horsham. Collected the Cortina, in which he followed me to Torrington

Common. We transferred her body to the boot of the Cortina, then drove to Brighton, where I left my car in a multi-storey car park a couple of streets from the flat where Miss da Sylva lived. Then I joined him in the Cortina and we set off for the New Forest. I wanted to bury her there. There's still a large part of the forest which is still blessedly untouched and peaceful: I thought it unlikely she'd be disturbed there. But . . . it didn't work out. We were stopped on the edge of the forest by a mobile policeman, and when we couldn't answer his questions to his satisfaction, he became suspicious. He insisted on looking in the boot. There was really nothing for it but to knock the poor fellow out and put his motorcycle and radio out of action.

'After that, it seemed senseless to continue on our way, so we turned round. We had no idea where we were going or how we were going to dispose of her corpse. We were getting desperate, when Percival suddenly remembered that his sister and her husband had a house not far away. It had been empty and up for sale for some years. Percival said it was unlikely to find a purchaser because it was beginning to fall into decay. There were several acres of unworked land at the back of the property, and we decided that would be the best place. Percival had no way of knowing that just that portion of land had already been sold — although he did fall over what I suppose was a boundary stake in the dark, but we couldn't tell what it was. We didn't worry about it, as we were in too much haste to be done with our task. At the time, he thought it must be a poacher's snare.

'At all events, that was where we laid her to rest. Then we went back to Brighton and drove the Cortina into her garage and locked it up. Then we walked to the car park, I got out my car, and we drove back to town. And that, I thought, I hoped, was the end of it. The next day I went off to Switzerland to carry out my role in the peace talks; and Willie Thompson, my bodyguard, was blown up in my place. It discomforts me greatly to think that if I'd taken the steps I was expected to take when I found Alys dead, it would not have been necessary for Willie Thompson to die. I mean they would not have had to make another attempt to get me out of the way.'

'Would you elucidate the point?' Mr. Gilbert said. 'Who are 'They'?'

'I'm not able to call them by name, but one of the Middle East terrorist organisations who wanted me out of the way at any price. Why they didn't make a direct attempt on my life that Saturday instead of killing Alys, I cannot imagine. Perhaps it seemed the easier way. Perhaps they had some reason for wishing to rid themselves of her too. I was meant of course to run to the police, and there would immediately have been a great hullabaloo in the press. I would have been pilloried, as John Profumo was long ago; and while this was going on, the whole delicate positioning of the peace talks would have slipped away and the opportunity lost, the moral issues overwhelmed in a wave of cynical laughter. This is really the 'quiet' method of the Soviet Union, which is usually so much more satisfactory in its effects than the violence of terrorism which only results in anger and a hardening of the will to resist. However, when the first way didn't produce the expected results, they turned swiftly to the way of violence. But again they failed: they got the wrong victim. I hope it's not out of place for me to mention that there was then nothing more they could do than wait until the attention of the press could be drawn to the matter.'

That concluded Edmund's testimony. It was followed by Mr. Boas's cross-examination; but it would be tedious to go over the same subject matter in all its minutiae again. Mr. Gilbert in his final speech included the dead woman in the plot against Edmund Burke, pointing out that it was she who had got in touch with him, she who had asked for the meeting, she who had chosen where they would eat and where they would stop afterwards. How else could the Mercedes which had followed them have known where to pick them up each time after it had been 'lost', unless it had been agreed between them beforehand?

Mr. Boas tried to destroy that line of argument in his final speech by calling the jury's attention to the fact that the only evidence for the existence of the black Mercedes had come from the accused himself.

Then came the judge's precise and careful summing up, concerned not with judging or justice but with the law. The jury retired.

Time crawled by. Very slowly.

Edmund could not complain. He had said what he wanted to say. His emotions were numbed. It no longer seemed to him, as far as he himself was concerned, to matter very much what the verdict would be one way or another. He had already lost almost everything that was important to him. Whatever the jury's decision, Edmund's public life was finished. It was over. He had lost. He would never be anything now but a private man with nothing more significant to attend to than the totally unimportant details of his private life, aims, and hopes. His world had shrunk to a pathetically narrow compass. There was the rest of his life to be got through: it yawned emptily before him.

He had struggled like a fly on flypaper, and all his desperate efforts had been for nothing. In the end the enemy had destroyed him. Or rather, he thought sharply, he had destroyed himself, had brought about his own downfall. He had supposed himself all along to be honest and sincere, above the lust for power, above pride and ambition and egotism. He thought he knew himself, but he'd been deceived. Yes, underneath all the while, 'the invisible worm's dark secret love did his life destroy'. The invisible worm of secret self-love was all the time gnawing at the roots of his life, destroying him.

Just for a moment, Edmund saw himself naked and was ashamed. He wanted to hide. He turned away, sickened. *That is what I am*, he thought. *That is what I really am, underneath the charm and friendliness and understanding.*

He would go back to his farm in the

Cotswolds and, like Candide, learn to cultivate his garden. There would be Cynthia. And Nicholas. It was more than he had any right to expect.

At the far end of the dark and endless tunnel confronting him, he caught the glimmer of a faint light. And suddenly he found himself caring quite desperately what the verdict would be. He was assailed by the anxiety that he might be found guilty after all. Why should he expect justice? And yet, the outcome was no longer a matter of indifference, because there were his wife and son to be considered. It would be too hard for them, too shameful, too wretched, to be left alone, perhaps for years, while he served his sentence. Nicholas would be ashamed of him, and Cynthia, feeling her youth flying past, would grow tired of waiting: and neither could be blamed. He thought with a pang that Nicholas would be grown up by the time he came out.

The sound of a bell pealing broke in on his thoughts.

'The jury is coming back now,' said the warder quite gently. 'We must go up.'

Edmund got to his feet, straightened himself and smoothed back his hair. Percival and his warder joined him. The two men exchanged a swift glance full of friendship and encouragement. Then with a tremor of apprehension, Edmund mounted the steps into the dock.

★ ★ ★

Mansoor Saliba greeted Naimeh Shehab formally with a salute, pinned on his breast the green ribbon of a Hero of the Liberation, and kissed him on both cheeks.

Shehab went off to celebrate as befits a hero. He was feeling very pleased with himself. He leaped up from the table suddenly, seeing the man with the drooping mustache from the house in Mornington Crescent.

'Ali! My friend! You are back again. Come and join us; we are making a little celebration. Here,' he said, proudly pointing at the ribbon on his chest, 'you see the reward for all my patient efforts.'

'What efforts were those, may one ask?'

'You know very well — the Englishman I was sent to destroy.'

'You mean Burke? I understood he was acquitted, wasn't he?'

'He was acquitted by his English law, but he was *destroyed*, my friend. He is now the ex-secretary of state for Mediterranean affairs, the ex-cabinet minister, the ex-member of parliament. A triumph of non-violence. I hope Ziadeh hears of it.'

'Two people dead. You call that non-violence?' said Ali, laughing, and banging him across the shoulders.

'Two people? But the man was killed by mistake. I planted the bomb to oblige Ziadeh, who was talking of reporting me for insubordination,' said Naimeh with a good-humoured smile. 'It was quite useless, you see; which simply proved my point. And the other one you can't count: it was only a woman and of no importance,' he explained, giving the woman he was embracing with one arm a little extra squeeze.

'But what are you saying to one another that is so funny?' the French girl said, pouting and half-laughing too.

358

'We were just saying, *ma petite poule*,' said Naimeh in an atrocious accent, 'that as women have no souls, as everyone knows, they are useful but of no importance at all.' And he delicately pinched her nipple between thumb and forefinger.

'*Ah ça enfin!* I should like very much to see how you would get on without us,' she mocked, making a very improper gesture with her hand. And they were all three laughing as they climbed the stairs to her little cubicle.

Leabharlanna Poibli Chathair Bhaile Átha Cliath
Dublin City Public Libraries

We do hope that you have enjoyed
reading this large print book.

Did you know that all of our titles
are available for purchase?

We publish a wide range of high
quality large print books including:
**Romances, Mysteries, Classics
General Fiction
Non Fiction and Westerns**

Special interest titles available in
large print are:
**The Little Oxford Dictionary
Music Book, Song Book
Hymn Book, Service Book**

Also available from us courtesy of
Oxford University Press:
**Young Readers' Dictionary
(large print edition)
Young Readers' Thesaurus
(large print edition)**

For further information or a free
brochure, please contact us at:
**Ulverscroft Large Print Books Ltd.,
The Green, Bradgate Road, Anstey,
Leicester, LE7 7FU, England.
Tel:** (00 44) **0116 236 4325
Fax:** (00 44) **0116 234 0205**

Other titles in the
Linford Mystery Library:

ON THE WORST DAY
OF CHRISTMAS

Tracey Walsh

When Bethany's childhood sweetheart Jake signs up to attend Chatham Hill School's Christmas reunion, she follows suit, despite her misgivings about returning to the eerie building. Arriving at the old school, Bethany notices something unusual about the reunion organiser — she looks considerably younger than she'd sounded over the phone. As the snow falls thicker, a disturbing fact becomes clear: only a few of the Class of '96 have not been told that the reunion is cancelled. Little do they know that even fewer of them will be allowed to leave . . .

MURDER AT CASTLE COVE

Charlotte McFall

When librarian Laurie decides that a literary festival is just what Castle Cove needs, it becomes clear that not everyone with an interest in the town agrees. As the festival gets underway, so do several sinister occurrences: threatening letters, missing manuscripts — and murder . . . When disreputable crime writer Suzie is sent to the festival, she resolves to blend into the background. But after she bumps into an old adversary and meets a new friend, she is sucked into the centre of a real mystery — one that she is determined to solve.